What the critics are saying:

"Once again, McCray's vibrant, pulsing characters and sizzling sex will thrill readers. Catie is an independent, tough and passionate woman, and Jarrod is a fantasy alpha male. Readers won't want to miss this one!" - *Cindy Whitesell, Romantic Times BOOKclub Magazine*

"Ms. McCray had done it again with WILDCAT! The instant, intense attraction between Catie and Jarrod is so well written, the reader can feel the heat. (Get ready for a very cold shower!) With many emotional twists and turns, as well as lots of hot sex, WILDCAT is a must read!" - *Maryellen Kunkel, Sensual Romance*

"Hold on to your hats, your hearts and your libidos…it's going to be a WILD ride! Cheyenne McCray is certainly proving to be one of erotica's best authors with blazing characters, riveting mystery and explosive scenes." - *Tracey West, The Road to Romance*

"Be sure to have something cold nearby as you read this, because WILDCAT is hot with a capital H! Nothing is sacred in the second installment of the Wild series by popular author Cheyenne McCray…" - *Courtney Bowden, Romance Reviews Today*

D1040434

Wildcat

Cheyenne McCray

WILDCAT
An Ellora's Cave Publication, November 2004

Ellora's Cave Publishing, Inc.
1337 Commerce Drive, Suite 13
Stow, OH 44236-0787

ISBN #1419950916

Other available format: MS Reader (LIT), Mobipocket (PRC)
Adobe (PDF), Rocketbook (RB), Mobipocket (PRC) & HTML

Edited by *Ann Richardson*
Cover art by *Darrell King*

Warning:

The following material contains graphic sexual content meant for mature readers. *Wildcat* has been rated *S-ensuous* by a minimum of three independent reviewers.

Ellora's Cave Publishing offers three levels of Romantica™ reading entertainment: S (S-ensuous), E (E-rotic), and X (X-treme).

S-*ensuous* love scenes are explicit and leave nothing to the imagination.

E-*rotic* love scenes are explicit, leave nothing to the imagination, and are high in volume per the overall word count. In addition, some E-rated titles might contain fantasy material that some readers find objectionable, such as bondage, submission, same sex encounters, forced seductions, etc. E-rated titles are the most graphic titles we carry; it is common, for instance, for an author to use words such as "fucking", "cock", "pussy", etc., within their work of literature.

X-*treme* titles differ from E-rated titles only in plot premise and storyline execution. Unlike E-rated titles, stories designated with the letter X tend to contain controversial subject matter not for the faint of heart.

Also by Cheyenne McCray:

Blackstar: *Future Knight*
Erotic Invitation
The Seraphine Chronicles: *Bewitched*
The Seraphine Chronicles: *Forbidden*
The Seraphine Chronicles: *Spellbound*
The Seraphine Chronicles: *Untamed*
Things That go Bump In the Night III
Vampire Dreams
Wild: *Wild Borders*
Wild: *Wildcard*
Wild: *Wildcat*
Wild: *Wildfire*
Wonderland: *King of Clubs*
Wonderland: *King of Diiamonds*
Wonderland: *King of Hearts*
Wonderland: *King of Spades*

Wildcat

To: Ann Richardson
My amazing editor who shares my
fondness for lemondrop martinis

Prologue

Catie Wilds pulled at her earlobe as she guided her battered ranch pickup into the parking lot of the Cochise County Sheriff's Department. She'd had it up to *here* with the damn cattle rustling, and she was determined to give the sheriff a piece of her mind.

After she parked, she stormed out of the pickup, slamming the door behind her. Catie had been pissed about Dean MacLeod's cattle being stolen, but now that the Wilds Ranch had been ripped off, it was definitely *personal*.

Shoving the glass doors open, Catie stomped into the reception area.

A busty brunette raised a sculpted eyebrow, her scarlet lips set in a what-the-hell-do-you-want smile. "May I help you?"

"I'd like to see Sheriff Savage." Catie propped her hands on her slim jean-clad hips. "Now."

"I don't think he's available." Boob Queen gave a don't-you-wish-he-was-available sniff as she picked up the phone. "Let me check."

Her temper escalating beyond eruption level, Catie glanced past the reception area. She looked into a room that was empty save for desks sporting computers and equipment...and that sorry excuse for a deputy, Ryan Forrester.

Without so much as a by-your-leave, Catie turned on her booted heel and headed straight for Forrester. She set her gaze on stun with shoot-to-kill as an alternative if the deputy didn't give her satisfaction.

"You can't…" Miss Mega-Tits spouted behind Catie.

"I need a word with you." Catie strode right up to Ryan, propped her hands on her hips, and frowned up at him. At only five foot four, she only came to the deputy's shoulder—but her glare was enough to cut down a man three times her size. And Catie knew how to wield her icy gaze like a sword.

Ryan's Adam's apple bobbed and he diverted his eyes, waving off Boob Woman, then turned his attention back to Catie. "What do you need, Cat?"

"I'll *tell* you what I need." Catie poked one finger at his deputy's star, punctuating each word with a jab at the metal. "I need my goddamned heifers back. I need you guys to get off your asses and figure out who the hell is stealing everyone's cattle."

Forrester stepped back. "We're working on it."

"Don't give me that crap." Catie advanced on the deputy as he retreated. "Get me the sheriff. *Now.*"

"What can I do for you?" A deep rumbling voice startled Catie out of her tirade and shivers shot down her spine.

She whipped her head to the side and her gaze locked with the most amazing crystalline green eyes—and the hottest man she'd ever seen. Her panties grew damp, every coherent thought fleeing her mind as she got lost in the pull of those magnetic eyes.

He had his hip and shoulder propped against the doorway of an office, his thumbs hooked in the pockets of his snug Wranglers, and a copper sheriff's star on his shirt. The man raised one hand to push up the brim of his tan felt Stetson as he studied her. His sable mustache twitched as he smiled, causing Catie's small nipples to harden into tiny torpedoes pointed straight at him.

Oh. My. God. For the first time in her life, Catie Wilds was speechless.

Sheriff Jarrod Savage studied the little wildcat who'd stormed into his office and ripped Deputy Forrester a new one. Damn she'd been cute as she'd spouted off at Forrester. Jarrod had enjoyed watching the flush in her fair cheeks, how her short blonde hair shimmered as she spoke and the way that sprinkling of freckles made her look so damn adorable.

He'd almost hated to interrupt her. And now...*well, hell.* The desire that sparked in those chocolate brown eyes charged up his own libido and it'd be a wonder if no one noticed the hardening in his cock. Something in his gut told him this was a woman worth getting to know — in every way a man could know a woman.

He pushed away from the door of his office and strode toward her. "Jarrod Savage," he said as he held out his hand.

Forrester mumbled something about "work to be done," and headed on out of the office, leaving Jarrod alone with the woman in the empty control room.

"Catie Wilds." The petite woman drew herself up and raised her chin as she took his hand.

Her vanilla musk teased his senses, along with the current sizzling between them as he took her hand in his. He wished he wasn't on duty so he could make things a little more personal between them. "A most definite pleasure, Catie Wilds."

As though remembering why she was there in the first place, the little spitfire pulled her hand from his and stepped back. "This cattle rustling bullshit has gone on long enough."

Jarrod nodded as he hooked his thumbs in his pockets. "You're telling me."

"Well, what do you intend to do about it?" Catie put her hands on her hips, that fiery glint back in her eyes. "We just lost fifteen heifers last night. We're one of the smaller ranches in the area, and that's something we sure as hell can't afford."

Frustration at their inability to track the bastards down was a fire in Jarrod's gut. "Believe me, we're putting everything and everyone we can on it."

"Obviously that's not good enough." Catie raised her chin. "What's it been? Six weeks since this whole mess started?"

Jarrod ran a hand over his mustache. "I know it's not what you want to hear, but we're working on it."

"Well, that's just *great*." The little wildcat spun on her heel and marched out of the control room.

He had to hold back a smile as he watched the natural sway of her slim hips as she headed out the front door, muttering something about, "Damn bureaucrats."

Jarrod shifted his position, trying to alleviate the new ache in his cock.

Looked like he'd have to pay a visit to the Wilds Ranch.

Chapter One

Catie Wilds checked the grandfather clock in the hallway and smiled. It was almost time for her *rendezvous*. Just the thought of what she was about to do made her feel naughty and absolutely delicious inside.

Wood floorboards creaked under her bare feet as she hurried to her bedroom. The old ranch house smelled of dust, lemon oil, and the single-serving lasagna she'd nuked in the microwave earlier. Unlike the modern MacLeod ranch house, Catie's home was well over a century old and looked every bit of it. But it was home.

When she reached her room, she closed the door in case her older brother Steve happened to come home early. The two had been running the ranch together since their father and his wife — number six — had been killed in a car accident, some five years ago.

And of course they hadn't seen their "real" mother since they were in elementary school. The woman had run off with a muscle-bound Mr. Arizona. Apparently that fling hadn't lasted, but good old "Mom" had enjoyed her freedom too much to get around to coming back home.

Catie pulled her pocketknife out and tossed it on her chest of drawers. She shimmied out of her jeans, her thoughts turning to the only person who'd even been close to being like a mom to her. Mrs. Karchner, who'd given Catie that pocketknife, used to own the ranch down the road from the Wilds. Mrs. Karchner had been the one stable person in Catie's wild youth. But the woman passed away a few years ago, breaking Catie's heart.

She sighed as she yanked her T-shirt over her head and tossed it onto the bed. She sure missed that woman.

After growing up in a broken family and witnessing too many failed marriages, Catie didn't believe in commitment. But she sure as hell believed in having as much fun as possible with the opposite sex.

Maybe she was too much like her mother.

Forcing the thoughts from her mind, Catie removed her bra and thong underwear and then pulled on a tiny jean skirt and a button-up blouse. She loved the feeling of being naked beneath her clothes, and it would make tonight's experience all the more fun. The jean material of her skirt felt rough and sexy against her bare skin and caused her pussy to throb and ache.

And since meeting the sexy new county sheriff yesterday, she'd been horny as all get out. Too bad she'd been pissed about the stolen cattle when she met that sex god of a cowboy. Or she'd have been tempted to jump the man. Well, for now she was putting aside any thought of rustling, money woes, and lack of a man with a good cock. She had a show to catch.

Once she had put on her leather moccasins, Catie slipped into the moonlit night that smelled crisp and clean from the rains of the past couple of days. Her nipples puckered and her heart beat a little faster as she picked her way through the tumbleweeds and mesquite bushes, out toward the cabin at the back of the ranch. Her moccasins made no sound as she stole along the slightly muddy path as quickly as she could.

She wanted to get there in time to watch *everything*.

And from the conversation she'd overheard this morning between Brad Taylor and the Wilson twins, there was going to be plenty to watch.

Catie had never spied on people having sex before, and she couldn't believe how turned-on she was just thinking about watching the three of them go at it. Well, there was that time she'd caught Dean MacLeod masturbating, and that had been erotic to watch from her hiding place in Dean's kitchen—and it had certainly whet her appetite for enjoying another bout of voyeurism.

Tumbleweeds scraped Catie's bare legs and an Arizona October breeze found its way underneath her mini skirt, straight to her bare pussy. It felt cool and erotic, and she was already incredibly wet. The sense of danger, coupled with the possibility of getting caught spying on one of the ranch hands in ménage à trois, heightened her excitement.

Catie had loved to play in the old cabin when she was a kid, and had kept the place in decent shape over the years as a kind of getaway when she wanted some time alone. When Brad had asked to use the cabin, she'd thought nothing of it—until she'd overheard his conversation with Sabrina and Sasha Wilson.

Even as Catie skirted the cabin to the back, she saw Brad's truck parked outside and heard feminine laughter from within. Damn, but she hoped she hadn't missed any of the good stuff.

She eased up to the back wall of the cabin, to a knothole that was just low enough that she had to bend over. Her skirt hiked up over her ass cheeks, and she felt the breeze on her pussy again as she peeked through the hole.

And got an eyeful.

* * * * *

Voices floated through the night air and Spirit's ears pricked toward the sound. Jarrod Savage brought the mare to a halt, and after listening for a moment, he swung down and let the reins drop to the ground. The mare was well-trained and intelligent, and wouldn't move unless Jarrod whistled to her.

Once he checked his utility belt and his firearm, Jarrod holstered the gun and quietly headed toward the sounds that were coming from a small cabin he could just make out in the moonlight.

For the past few weeks, despite what one Miss Catie Wilds might think, he'd been investigating a rash of cattle rustling that had escalated in this part of the state. As the new county sheriff, Jarrod's reputation was riding on getting this case solved, and getting it solved *now*.

He eased through the dry grass and tumbleweeds, his hand resting on his weapon's grip, his senses on high alert, on the lookout for the slightest indication of danger.

The flash of white caught Jarrod's eye and he froze. His eyes narrowed as he watched the small figure stealing through the night, to the back of the cabin. When the figure moved up to the wall, light from inside the cabin shone on her face.

A woman. A damn beautiful…and a familiar woman at that.

Jarrod grinned as he realized it was that little spitfire of a rancher who'd come storming into his office yesterday. Catie Wilds had more than piqued his interest.

His cock had been on full-throb every time he'd thought about her since.

And as she bent over to peek into a hole in the wall of the cabin, Catie's short blonde hair swung forward. Her next-to-nothing-skirt   hiked   up—the   moonlight illuminating her completely naked ass and pussy.

Despite years of law enforcement training and plenty of practice in keeping emotionally and physically detached from his work, Jarrod couldn't help but feel a stirring in his cock. He swallowed, hard, as Catie licked her lips and began fondling her breasts while she looked through the hole, into the cabin.

Feminine laughter came from inside the cabin, and then a woman's voice said, "Lick my pussy, Brad."

Jarrod's mouth turned up into a grin. The perky little blonde was a dang Peeping Tom. Or rather a Peeping Tomasina.

His cock grew even harder as he watched her move one hand beneath her skirt while her other hand continued to pluck one nipple through her blouse.

Damn, but he had to get his mind back on his job and off the hot woman in front of him. The woman who looked like she was dying to get fucked.

* * * * *

Catie's breath caught as she watched Brad, who stood in the center of the cabin, licking Sabrina's huge nipples. Sasha was on her knees, sucking on Brad's cock and fondling his balls. "You're so good at giving head, sugar," Brad said in between mouthfuls of Sabrina's breasts.

Sabrina and Sasha were identical twins with long black hair and almond-shaped brown eyes. They both had large breasts that Catie would've killed for, along with generous curves that Catie envied — so unlike her own petite, compact, and athletic figure. The only difference between the twins was the small mole on Sabrina's left cheek, otherwise Catie would never be able to tell them apart.

Catie moved her hands to her own breasts as she watched Brad suckle Sabrina's nipples. The woman slipped her hands into Brad's hair and cried out as he nipped her.

"Eat me, Brad," Sabrina demanded.

Brad rumbled something low that Catie couldn't hear. But then Brad moved to the lone bed across the room from the peephole, and lay flat on his back. With a sexy grin, he motioned for the twins to join him. Sasha giggled, and climbed onto the bed. She knelt between his thighs and resumed sucking his cock while Sabrina straddled Brad, her clit right over his mouth.

Catie moved one hand beneath her skirt to her own pussy and slipped her fingers inside of her wet folds. As she watched Sabrina grinding her hips against Brad's face, Catie stroked her clit. She was so aroused that if she wasn't careful, she'd come before she even got started.

Well, what was the matter with that? Wasn't that what multiple orgasms were for?

She bit down on her lip, holding back a moan, as her motions increased. The night smelled of piñon and sage, and she smelled her own desire. She even imagined she caught the scent of sex coming from within the cabin.

Sabrina pinched and pulled her nipples as she demanded, "Lick me harder, dammit!"

Catie could feel her orgasm building. Winding up inside of her, tighter and tighter.

Sabrina screamed as she hit her peak. "Yes! God, yes!"

Not a second later, Catie's own climax rushed through her like a warm desert wind. Her body shuddered as she continued to stroke her clit, drawing out her orgasm—

A hand clamped over her mouth and another around her waist.

Catie froze, her heart pounding and her blood rushing as her orgasm-dazed mind fought to figure out what the hell was happening. Her body was still trembling from her climax and a rush of fear added to the convulsions.

"You like to watch people fuck?" a man's deep voice murmured next to her ear, a husky whisper that sent an odd thrill straight to her core.

She couldn't move. Could barely think.

"Do you?" His tone was so low, rich and sensual that Catie's knees went weak as she nodded. Was there something familiar about his voice?

The man's hat brushed against her hair as he moved his body closer. She caught his masculine scent along with the faint odor of mint. And when he pressed his body to hers, she felt his cock through his jeans, hard against her bare ass.

Ohmigod. The man's cock was *huge.*

Despite the fact the man was probably a stranger, and currently had her trapped in his grip, Catie felt her core flooding with moisture.

"Look at them." The man's voice was hoarse, like he was almost too aroused to talk. "Does that turn you on?"

Catie's gaze went back to the threesome in the cabin and her eyes widened. Sabrina was on her hands and knees, Brad behind her, his cock pressed to her ass. Sasha straddled Sabrina backwards. He thumbed Sasha's clit with one hand while holding onto Sabrina's hip with the other.

"Fuck me!" Sabrina cried. Brad yanked her ass toward him and slid his cock into her pussy.

"Would you like to be fucked right now?" the stranger asked as Brad pounded into Sabrina while he stroked Sasha's clit with his thumb.

Catie caught her breath as the man kept his hand over her mouth, and moved his other hand down between her thighs. Even though she didn't know who had her in his grip, and even though she had *never* had sex with anyone she didn't know, Catie was so turned-on that she wanted to shout, *Yes! Take me, now!*

But the stranger didn't wait for an answer. He slid his fingers over her mound and into her slit as she watched Brad fucking Sabrina.

"Mmmm, smooth. I like a shaved pussy." The stranger's voice was a silken whisper as he caressed Catie's clit, his calloused fingers exerting the perfect motion, perfect pressure. "Damn but you're wet." He slid his fingers into her core. "And so tight. I'd bet we'd be a good fit."

A gasp rose up within Catie at the incredible feel of his fingers inside her and his jean-clad cock pressed tight against her backside.

"What do you think, little wildcat?" The man started back on her clit, stroking it, and Catie moaned behind his hand. "I bet you taste real good, too."

Catie trembled with a hurricane of desire as the man nuzzled her neck, his mustache brushing her soft skin as he pressed his firm lips to her. She could just imagine how that mustache would tickle her thighs as he licked her clit. Mustache...who did she know that wore a mustache?

"You smell like vanilla...and musk." The stranger moved his lips to the hair behind her ear and she shuddered. "Good enough to eat."

From inside the cabin, Sabrina screamed with another orgasm.

"My turn. Fuck me, Brad." Sasha lay on her back, her black hair splayed across the old bed quilt. Brad slid between her thighs and pummeled her with his cock.

Wanton feelings rose and spiraled throughout Catie, unlike anything she'd every felt before. On and on the stranger stroked her, murmuring erotic words, until the most intense orgasm she'd ever felt exploded through her. A scream of pleasure threatened to tear from her, but the man kept his hand tight against her mouth, holding back the sound. Her body shuddered and rocked against the stranger's as he continued to finger her, drawing out her climax until she couldn't take anymore.

In her orgasmic haze, Catie was dimly aware that the man had released his hold on her. She braced one hand on the cabin wall, took a deep breath, and turned to look at the man who'd given her the most incredible orgasm of her life—

Only to discover he'd vanished into the night.

* * * * *

Gritting his teeth, Jarrod eased back through the darkness to where he'd left his mare. He raised his fingers to his nose and smelled Catie's scent on his hand, which was definitely a mistake—his cock grew harder yet, if that was even possible. Thoughts of her consumed him...of tasting her, driving his cock into her, and making her scream with orgasm after orgasm.

When Jarrod reached his mare, he paused to look back toward the cabin. It was too dark and too far to see if Catie was still there. Yet somehow he knew she hadn't left. That she was looking into the night, trying to see *him*.

Damn but he couldn't get the beautiful woman out of his mind. He should have sunk his cock into her, branding her and made her his woman. Even though she probably didn't know who he was, he knew she'd wanted him as much as he'd wanted her—there was some kind of connection between them that was, dammit, *electric*. But no, he'd walked away out of an outmoded sense of chivalry and duty.

Jarrod's cock throbbed against his zipper, and no amount of shifting eased the pressure. Crickets chirruped and he could still hear the faint sound of voices and laughter from the trio going at it in the cabin. A cool breeze brought scents of the desert to him, and he almost imagined he smelled the woman's vanilla musk scent.

Well, hell. He wasn't going to get anywhere at this rate. Jarrod was so horny that he could barely walk straight, much less saddle up and ride.

Spirit swatted her tail against her flank, the swish of wiry hair brushing Jarrod's arm. He unbuckled his belt, eased his zipper down, and pulled his cock out of his briefs. Imagining he was sliding into Catie's sweet core, he stroked his dick from base to tip. Yeah, he could just picture that hot little body, thighs spread wide and showing him her shaved pussy.

While he stared into the night, toward where he'd left the woman, his motions increased as he remembered her smell, the feel of her ass pressed against his cock. His body tensed, his balls drew up and heat flooded him from his Stetson to his steel-toed boots. Jarrod gritted back a groan as he came, his semen arcing onto the tumbleweeds. He continued stroking himself until he'd milked out every last bit of come.

Shaking his head, he slipped his cock back into his briefs and fastened his jeans and belt. He didn't remember being that horny since he was a teenager—and he'd certainly never made a woman come while on the job, or even jacked himself off while doing investigative work.

Jarrod mounted Spirit and guided the mare away from the ranch and back toward where he'd left his truck and horse trailer. He may have walked away from Catie tonight, but come tomorrow, he'd find her and stake his claim.

And next time he intended to do a lot more than make her come.

Chapter Two

The front door slammed, the reverberations rattling through the house and waking Catie. She blinked away early morning sunlight as wisps of her dream came back to her — of a dark stranger with a very impressive cock.

Her nipples peaked beneath the sheet and her pussy ached at the thought of what had happened last night to inspire such an erotic dream. Catie smiled and stretched her limbs, the sheet sliding across her bare flesh and down to her waist, exposing her nipples to the cool morning air. She always slept in the nude and loved how freshly laundered linens smelled, and how they felt against her naked skin.

With a grin, Catie bounded out of bed and snatched her robe off the hook on the back of her bedroom door. She was a morning person and rarely slept in late, but that dream had certainly been worth sleeping in for.

She slipped on her robe and then opened her door to head to the bathroom across the hall, her mind wandering to the memory of last night. How incredible it felt to have the stranger's muscled body pressed tight to her backside, his big hand between her thighs, his fingers inside her and stroking her clit. And *god*, that deep, sexy voice of his was enough to make her come just thinking about it.

Too bad the man had pulled a vanishing act. She had a feeling he would've been one hell of a ride. His voice, though. Something about it had been familiar. Was he someone she knew? He had a mustache, wore jeans and a western hat—that much she'd been able to tell. She knew a few men with mustaches...Kev Grand and a couple of Dean MacLeod's ranch hands...but the voice just didn't match any of them.

Catie shut and locked the bathroom door as she thought about how she'd instinctively trusted her mystery man. She had a natural intuition about most folks that was damn near always dead-on. The one time she didn't listen to that internal voice, she came damn close to being raped in high school by an asshole named Reggie Parker. Thank God Steve had come to her rescue and kicked Reggie's skinny white ass.

Unfortunately, Steve had ended up in jail overnight for hitting a minor. That bastard Reggie had deserved having his face turned into hamburger. Catie still owed her big brother for that one.

The faucet creaked and pipes groaned as Catie ran the water in the tub, waiting for it to turn from freezing to only chilly before she jumped in. She and her brother Steve needed to get a new water heater in the worst way, but right now all their cash was sunk into the herd. If only the price of beef would go back up, they might be able to afford a thing or two. The smell of rust met her nose, the water coming out orangish-red, compliments of plumbing twice her age. New pipes would be nice, too. Hell, a new house was what they really needed.

Once the water ran clear, Catie ditched her robe and stepped under the spray. She shivered, her nipples forming hard knots from the cold. Accustomed to rushing through her morning ice-water shower, she shampooed her hair, soaped her body, and shaved her armpits, legs, and pussy, in record time.

When she was just about finished with her shower, Catie ran her fingers between her thighs, remembering how the stranger enjoyed touching her, and how he'd said he liked a shaved pussy. She liked the way her skin felt, too, satiny smooth beneath her fingertips. Tilting her head back, she slid her fingers into her slit and stroked her hard nub as cold water rained on her back.

What would he look like? She moved her free hand to one breast and began tweaking her nipple as she tried to picture the man. Judging by the height of his cock pressed against her backside, she figured he was a good eight inches taller than her, which would put him at close to six feet.

Her fingers moved faster, stroking her clit, her body growing warmer despite the chill of the water on her flesh. His cock had felt thick and long—it had to have been at least ten inches. It would feel so good plunging in and out of her pussy, filling her, stretching her as they fucked.

The sound of water roared in Catie's ears, blending with the pounding of her heart as she drew herself closer to the summit. Her body jerked and she yelped as she reached climax, her head spinning while goose bumps sprouted on her skin.

After she had drawn out her orgasm as long as possible, Catie shut off the water and reached for a towel off the rack. Damn, but she loved orgasms. Definitely no such thing as too many.

* * * * *

It was late afternoon by the time Catie was close to finishing her daily chores in the barn behind the old ranch house. The sun hung low over the Mule Mountains and the air smelled of fall, mixed with barn smells of dust, manure and alfalfa hay.

Humming softly to herself, Catie raked out Sassafras's stall. Sass was a dappled appaloosa mare that more than lived up to her name, but to Catie the ten-year-old horse was like a member of the family. Sass had distinctive cream-colored knee-high stockings on her front legs, but her back legs were solid chocolate brown, as was most of her coat where she didn't have cream spots. A diamond blaze was on her sleek muzzle, and she had a mischievous spark in her intelligent brown eyes.

Catie loved to ride whenever she got the chance. It had been her favorite activity as she was growing up. Her way to escape the world and her fucked up family life. She'd done pretty well in rodeo competitions, even beating Dean MacLeod a few times in barrel racing.

A few stalls down from Sass was Shadow Warrior, a champion stallion they'd had for eight years. They'd had to sell the rest of their horses when things got tough and they couldn't afford the feed or maintenance any longer. Warrior they used primarily for stud service, a way to add a little cash to their income. And Sass, well, there was no way in hell Catie would ever let her go.

The mare hung her head over the side of the next stall and lipped Catie's short blonde hair. "Cut that out." She grinned and shooed Sass away with a playful pat on the mare's muzzle. Sass whickered and tossed her head, acting for all the world like she was laughing at Catie.

The entire morning, all Catie had been able to think about was the stranger who'd brought her to orgasm last night. She had never let *any* man under her skin, and it was starting to irk her that she couldn't get one little sorta-sexual encounter off her mind. Maybe it was the fact that all he had done was finger-fuck her, and then he'd vanished into the night.

Yeah, that was it. Curiosity at what it might be like to actually have sex with the man. The man who had a voice so deep and sensual it sent shivers through her just thinking about it. The man who'd obviously had a cock big enough to please.

After Catie's experience with the stranger, even Jess Lawless, Dean MacLeod's new foreman, didn't seem half as intriguing as before—and Jess was one hot cowboy, with an incredibly sexy drawl. Catie had been flirting with Jess since she met him, but for some reason he'd kept his distance. She might be forward, but she didn't outright chase any man. No man was worth *that* much trouble.

Tingles skittered along Catie's spine and she stopped raking as the thought of another incredible hunk crossed her mind.

It couldn't have been *him*. Could it?

Day before yesterday, when she'd met Jarrod Savage, the new sheriff, she'd soaked her panties the instant she'd laid eyes on him. She hadn't been able to speak at first, she'd been so totally captured by lust. He had the most amazing crystalline green eyes, an incredibly deep and thrilling voice, and the sexiest mustache...

Dogs barking and the sound of a truck driving up to the ranch jerked Catie from her fantasizing. She propped the rake up against the stall door, pulled off her leather work gloves and tossed them onto a hay bale. Wiping her hands on her jeans, she stomped her boots on the hard-packed dirt floor to kick loose some of the manure.

"Be right back, girl." Catie patted Sass's neck and headed toward the open barn door.

She paused in the shadows, and her heart rate picked up when she saw a truck with the county sheriff's logo park in her front yard. And then a warm flush stole over her as that fine-looking lawman climbed out of it…Jarrod Savage, the new county sheriff.

Oh. My. God.

It couldn't have been him last night.

Damn — it had to be.

As she watched the sheriff stride from the truck, Catie tugged on her ear, a nervous habit she'd had since she was a child. Sheriff Savage walked up to her brother, Steve, who was standing in front of the house.

He smiled and shook hands with Savage, and Catie wished she was closer so that she could hear what they had to say. If she wasn't so sweaty and didn't smell like the barn, she would have strolled right out. She wanted more of what she knew that sheriff could give her.

Damn, but that lawman was one hot hunk of male. Tall, broad shoulders, narrow hips and a tight ass. She had a side view of him, and couldn't tell what color his hair was because of his Stetson, but he had a sexy sable mustache and nice big hands. She liked a man with big —

As if aware of her, Savage looked straight to where she was hidden in the shadows. The world stopped on its axis, and for one long moment, she all but forgot how to breathe.

Prickling erupted at Catie's nape and the fine hairs stood up on her arms.

He couldn't see her, could he?

Her heart beat faster as his eyes seemed to lock with hers. But then he turned back to Steve and continued talking like nothing strange had just happened.

Nothing *had* happened. Surely it was just her desire and thoughts of what happened last night that was making her crazy.

Catie eased back into the barn, her skin tingling. Her normal I-don't-give-a-damn-what-anyone-thinks attitude had suddenly taken a hike. She was sweaty, probably had dirt streaked across her face and smelled like a horse—not to mention the horseshit. As much as she was dying to get to know that sexy lawman, now was *not* the right time.

Biting her bottom lip, Catie yanked on her gloves and set back to work, determined not to sneak another peek at the gorgeous man outside.

Sass whickered and moved her head up and down in a kind of horsey nod, as though telling Catie she should go out and see him anyway.

Catie glared at her. "What do you know?" she muttered. "You're just a horse."

In response, Sass snorted and blew snot all over Catie's shirt.

"Brat." Catie swiped at it with her gloves and managed to wipe the worst of it off. "See if you get your sugar lump later."

* * * * *

He'd found her.

Jarrod knew it deep in his gut that Catie was there as soon as he'd driven up to the Wilds Ranch. While he talked to Steve Wilds about the rash of cattle rustling that had struck other ranchers in the area, Jarrod's instincts had kicked in. And then he'd *felt* Catie watching him from the barn.

He pushed up the brim of his hat and turned his attention back to Wilds. "Anything unusual happen on your property that you're aware of?" Jarrod asked, watching Wilds for any sign of recognition or discomfort at the questioning. "Anything at all?"

"Other than losing fifteen head of cattle the other night?" Wilds shook his head, his manner calm and amiable. "Nothing more than the fence being cut a couple of times. Between the Flying M and our ranch. Jess Lawless, the foreman over at Flying M, he's been riding the line just like me, but we can't catch the bastards in action. "

Jarrod nodded. "Mind if I talk with your sister?"

With a shrug, Wilds jerked his thumb in the direction of the barn. "Cat's probably working with her appaloosa."

After thanking Wilds and shaking the man's hand again, Jarrod strode toward the barn. Blood thrummed in his veins, the same feeling he always got when he was close to solving a case. For over ten years he'd been a street cop and then a detective with the Tucson Police Department. He'd served with TPD from the time he was a rookie until he'd decided to move to the southeastern corner of Arizona to take over as Sierra Vista's Chief of Police, some six years ago.

Needing a new challenge, Jarrod had decided to run for Cochise County Sheriff and the previous fall had beat out the troubled incumbent, John "Bull" Stevens, by a hefty margin. The papers were making a bid deal over the cattle rustling, and Jarrod was determined to seek out the culprits and lock the bastards up.

In a few strides, he made it to the open barn door. Even before he walked into the barn, Jarrod heard the sound of a rake scraping against the ground and a horse's soft whicker. When he entered, he stopped for a moment, allowing his eyes to adjust to the dimness. His gaze immediately focused on the petite blonde who had her back to him and was raking out a stall.

Jarrod smiled and his cock jerked to attention. He would recognize that fine little ass anywhere...even clothed.

The appaloosa raised its head and eyed Jarrod, but Catie didn't seem to realize he was there. Just like last night.

He eased up behind her and caught the scent of her vanilla musk, mixed with her own unique smell. "Hello, Catie Wilds."

Catie gave a small shriek and whirled around. She clenched the rake to her chest, her big brown eyes wide. "What the hell did you sneak up on me for?" She raised her chin and took a step back. "You like to have scared the crap out of me."

Damn, but she was cute, right down to the sprinkling of freckles across her nose, and Jarrod couldn't help but grin. "You gonna hit me with that thing?"

She glanced at the rake handle and back at him. "Depends."

Jarrod raised an eyebrow. "On what?"

"If you ever do that again."

As she stared up at the man, Catie took a deep breath and tried to calm her scattered thoughts and the pounding of her heart. *Omigod*, it was him. That incredible voice and those mesmerizing crystal green eyes...she was definitely in lust.

"Why don't we try this again." His mustache twitched as he smiled and held out his hand. "It's good to see you again Ms. Wilds."

"Ms. Wilds?" She propped the rake against the stall door, pulled off her gloves and tucked them into her back pocket. "Don't you think we're a little beyond that, Sheriff Savage?"

"Yeah." He took her hand, and damn if his touch didn't send tingles straight to her pussy. "After last night, I hope you'll just call me Jarrod."

His eyes swept over her, lingering on her aroused nipples poking against her thin T-shirt. Her breasts were small enough that she didn't feel the need to wear a bra all the time, and right now she felt almost naked under his gaze.

Catie, who had never found herself at a loss for words around a man, once again couldn't think of a thing to say, just like the first time she'd met him in his office. Her body vibrated with awareness and need, and all she wanted to do was get naked with him. *Now.*

"Well?" He released her hand and brought his fingers to her face. She felt him lightly brushing dirt away from her cheek. "What do you say?"

She leaned into the touch of his hand against her face. "Yes."

Jarrod cocked an eyebrow and cupped her chin with his hand. "Yes...what?"

"Whatever you're asking," she murmured, her eyes focused on his, "the answer's yes."

A slow, sexy smile crept over his face, and his voice dropped to that seductive pitch that made her knees weak and her panties oh-so-wet. "If I wanted to kiss you, that'd be all right?"

Catie brought her hand up to the copper sheriff's star pinned to his shirt, and traced it with her finger. "Damn straight."

He moved closer, so that his muscled body was a fraction from hers, so close she could feel the heat of him through her T-shirt and jeans. "What if I said I wanted to fuck you, Catie? Right here in the barn. You'd say yes?"

She kept her gaze locked with his as she placed her hand right on the bulge beneath his jeans, giving him his answer. He sucked in his breath as she trailed her fingernails up and down his impressive length. God he was big, and did she *ever* want him.

Jarrod dropped his hand from her face as he fought to control the lust building up within him. "If you're not careful, little wildcat, I might just take you up on what you're offering."

"Oh?" Catie's chocolate brown eyes sparkled with sensuality. "What's stopping you?"

"Only the fact that I'm on the job." He resisted the urge to taste those sweet lips that pursed into a sexy smile. "And the fact that your brother and someone else are real close to walking in on us." He jerked his head toward the barn door to where he heard the sound of voices coming closer.

"Ah." She lowered her hand from his crotch and grinned. "Works for me."

"About that 'yes'..." Jarrod stepped away, putting some distance between them before unwelcome company arrived. "Dinner tomorrow night—I'll pick you up at seven."

She didn't even hesitate. "What should I wear?"

And neither did he. "Exactly what you had on last night."

Catie shivered as Jarrod moved away from her to the barn door to talk with Steve and the man she had formerly lusted over, Jess Lawless, the Flying M Ranch foreman. Catie couldn't help but enjoy the view as she watched the gorgeous sheriff talk with Jess and Steve. Jess was another example of prime U.S. male with dark brown hair, blue eyes that could make a woman beg, a Bruce Willis adorable grin and a sexy drawl that would soak a gal's panties.

Yet now that she'd met Jarrod Savage, Catie didn't even feel a twinge of lust for Jess anymore. Well, that was strange. She'd never had any problem maintaining multiple lustings before.

"Someone tried to steal Dean MacLeod's new prize bull again," Jess was saying to Jarrod. "Imp. The yearling. Damn near caught the bastard in the act, but he got away on horseback. Again."

Catie's attention snapped from thoughts of fucking the sheriff to concern for her friend's ranch. She walked up to the men, feeling like a pixie in the land of the giants. "Is Imp all right?"

Jess looked down at Catie and gave her that grin of his that used to make her knees feel like gelatin. "Hey there, Catie." His friendly smile vanished as he answered her question. "Yeah, the little shit is fine. But that's the second attempt this week. Somebody's got a real hard-on for that bully-boy. Guess because he'd fetch a helluva price."

He turned back to Steve and Jarrod. "Dean MacLeod left town for a week with Jake Reynolds. My thinking is that the thief knew she was out of town, so that's why he picked last night to strike again, not counting on me being around."

"Their trip sure was sudden-like," Jarrod murmured.

Steve shook his head, laughter in his brown eyes. "Well, if you'd seen those two before they left…my guess is they've found themselves a hotel room and won't be seeing daylight for a while."

Jess snickered. "Ain't that the truth."

Catie had to laugh, too. The last time she'd seen Dean was at dinner a couple of nights ago, and Jake had come storming in only to throw Dean over his shoulder and practically kidnap her. Steve, Jess, and Catie had been left alone to finish dinner and clean up the mess—not that anyone complained. The men were more than happy to polish off every bite of the enchiladas. Dean had called briefly to say that she and Jake were going on a little trip, and she'd call when they returned.

Jarrod smiled, but his expression went serious again. "So there's a good chance that the perp is someone who's around enough to know what's going on at the ranch."

With a nod, Jess replied, "Yeah. But the question remains—is this stuff with Imp tied to the rustling, or is it a separate deal?"

"All these times, no one got a good look at the fella?" Steve asked as he took off his western hat and ran a hand through his thick blonde hair.

Jess frowned. "No, damn it. This morning I followed the tracks up into the mountain range behind the Flying M, but lost 'em once I got to the running water. There's been so much rain the past couple of days that all the washes are full, and it was easy for him to hide his horse's tracks by staying in the water."

"Why don't I head over to the MacLeod ranch with you?" Jarrod stroked his hand over is mustache and Catie imagined what it would feel like to have that hand stroking her, instead. "I'd like to check everything out myself."

Lawless stiffened, like he'd taken offense, but he said, "Suit yourself. Check out whatever you want, but I've given it a real thorough once over."

Check out whatever you want. Catie studied Sheriff Godbody. *No shit. Can't wait to check out every inch of* that.

Jarrod's eyes met Catie's and for a moment she was sure he'd read her mind. He smiled and tipped his hat. "See you later, Catie Wilds."

Chapter Three

"You're *what*, Dean?" Catie damn near dropped the phone onto the kitchen floor, unable to believe what her best friend had just said.

"Married." The excitement in Dean's voice was unmistakable. "And please call me Dee now — that's what Jake calls me."

"Dee. Christ. Whatever. All right. Dee it is." Catie held her hand to forehead, still trying to process her friend's news. "So when? How?"

"Jake and I took off for Las Vegas the night you came over for dinner. You know, when the big lug threw me over his shoulder and sorta kidnapped me."

Catie was sure she heard Jake in the background, murmuring something like "Not. lug. You mean *desperado*."

"When you called the next day, you said you two were staying out of town for a week." Catie pulled her pocketknife from her jeans and flicked it open and closed. Open and closed. "I figured Jake had taken you on a trip or something. But I had no idea you were going off to get *married*."

"*Jake*. Not now." Dean — make that Dee — giggled and Catie rolled her eyes, imagining the sickly-sweet newlywed crap going on at the other end of the line. "Anyway," she continued into the phone, "You're the first person that I've told."

Even though she was dead-set against marriage, Catie crammed her pocketknife in her jeans and tried to muster up enthusiasm for her friend who sounded so happy, and put a smile in her voice. "Tell that cowboy he'd better take good care of you, or I'll kick his ass."

"I'll let him know." Laughter bubbled up from Dee. "Now can you come to our reception next Saturday? We're having a barbeque and dance here at the ranch."

"Well, of course." Catie held the phone with one hand and tugged at her earlobe with her other as she did her best to put some enthusiasm into her voice. "You know I wouldn't miss it."

"Great. Be here at noon." Dee sighed, a sound of contentment. She was so damn happy, that Catie couldn't help but feel pleasure for her friend. "What's new with you, sweetpea?"

I'm planning to fuck the sheriff, and I can't wait. Catie's body warmed at the mere thought, and she clenched her thighs together to ease the ache blooming in her pussy.

"I'm going out tomorrow night with Jarrod Savage," she said aloud.

"The Sheriff?" Dee's voice perked up. "I've met him — talk about one hell of a sexy man. I just knew you'd find him hot. Promise to give me all the juicy details."

"Don't I always?" Catie's smile was wistful as she imagined that their nightlong girl gabfests had come to an abrupt end with Dee's getting shackled.

After they said their goodbyes, Catie punched the phone off and set it on the countertop.

Married. What the hell was Dee thinking? Catie shook her head. It had been good to hear Dee's excitement and joy, but Catie just hoped her friend had made the right decision and would be happy — Dee deserved that and more.

But as far as Catie was concerned, marriage was a mistake she was damn sure she would *never* make.

* * * * *

Jarrod tossed the manila folder onto his cluttered wooden desk and settled back in his chair. A frown creased his face as he stared out the glass window of his office and into the busy control room of the county sheriff's department. It was the morning after running into his little wildcat, and he was having a hell of a time getting his mind on the job. He disliked the paperwork end of being sheriff, preferring fieldwork, so he delegated what office duties he could.

And thoughts of what he wanted to do with Catie Wilds sure beat the heck out of signing dozens of documents or trying to catch a gang of thieves.

ʼ He remembered how she'd come storming into his office, her eyes blazing and how she'd laid into one of his deputies, Ryan Forrester. She'd looked so damn fiery and sexy that Jarrod had just stood and watched her carry on for at least a minute or two.

"Sheriff?" Forrester's voice cut into Jarrod's thoughts, forcing him back to the cattle rustling puzzle at hand.

He glanced from his desktop to the sandy-haired deputy who stood in the open doorway of his office. "Yeah?"

Forrester stepped into the room and hooked his thumbs in his front pockets. The armpits of his tan uniform were sweat-soaked, and perspiration coated the man's upper lip. "Rustlers made off with another couple dozen head of cattle last night."

"Damn." Jarrod slammed his hand on his desk and stood so abruptly he knocked his chair over, its thump like an exclamation point to his frustration. "This has been going on for two months. And that's two months too long."

"Uh-huh." Forrester's gaze dropped to the manila folder on Jarrod's desk. "What's your opinion on the Kev Grand connection?"

Jarrod reached for the file and flipped it open. "Not much here. Jess Lawless, the MacLeod foreman, found a pair of wire cutters that belong to Grand, next to downed fence line — Grand admits to owning those cutters." Jarrod ran his finger down the page. "You've discovered a portion of the MacLeod herd mixed in with Grand's, but since their properties border one another, that's not so surprising."

Stroking his hand over his mustache, Jarrod thought out loud, "This Jess Lawless just happens to start working for Dean MacLeod around the same time the rustling started. And he was none too happy with me poking around the Flying M the other day."

"What about Steve Wilds?"

Jarrod's gaze shot up to meet Forrester's icy blue eyes. "What about him?"

Forrester shrugged. "Steve's been short on cash for awhile. The ranch is in the red, so he has motive to earn a little money on the side. And he seems to have a bunch of cash all of a sudden."

Frowning, Jarrod closed the manila folder. "Any proof?"

"A lady friend of mine works at the bank in Douglas." The deputy shifted and folded his arms across his chest. "She said Wilds made a big deposit a couple of days ago — a good chunk of change."

With a sigh, Jarrod scrubbed his hand over his mustache. "See what you can dig up."

When the deputy left his office, Jarrod righted his chair and sank into it. If Catie's brother ended up being a suspect, that sure put a damper on things. Hell, Catie could be involved for all Jarrod knew.

But his gut told him otherwise, and unless his lust for her was screwing with his instinct, he was sure she was innocent. Steve Wilds, on the other hand, could very well be in the mess well past the crown of his Stetson.

* * * * *

The sound of a truck driving up to the ranch house jerked Catie's heart into full gear. She dodged into her bedroom, chiding herself for being excited about a date. It had been years since she'd been nervous about going out, but there was something about Jarrod that made her body tingle just thinking about the man.

Catie smoothed her short jean skirt as she checked her reflection in the mirror. She was wearing the same skirt as the night she met Jarrod, but she'd chosen a hot pink strapless top that bared her flat belly and slender shoulders.

She pushed her blonde hair behind her ears and put a touch of gloss on her lips. A knock sounded at the door at the same time she spritzed on her vanilla musk cologne. After grabbing her jean jacket, she hurried to the door, only to see Steve walking in with Jarrod.

Her pulse skyrocketed at the sight of Jarrod, who was wearing a snug shirt that showed his cut physique to perfection and tight Wranglers that molded his muscular thighs — and showed a promising bulge.

Steve frowned, took off his western hat and tossed it onto the hat rack, then ran his fingers through his blonde hair. "You didn't tell me you had a date with the Sheriff, Cat."

"Since when do I tell you about any of my dates?" She looked past Steve and smiled at Jarrod. "Hey there."

"Hey yourself." Jarrod touched the brim of his Stetson and smiled at Catie.

"I'm gonna grab myself some eats." Steve nodded toward the kitchen, a tired, irritated look in his eyes. "Catch you later."

As Steve vanished into the kitchen, Jarrod murmured, "You look like spring come early."

She returned his smile with a sassy toss of her head, letting her gaze rake over him. Her voice was husky as she met his eyes. "I'd say you look like a real good reason to come…early."

A growl practically rumbled from his chest, and his green eyes darkened from crystal to almost jade. "Let's go."

Catie slipped on her jacket and headed out the front door as Jarrod held it open for her. The cool night smelled clean and crisp, the sky clear with stars spattered across its expanse.

"You've got a choice to make," he said as they walked to the black truck parked out front.

She paused in front of the passenger door and looked up at him. "I told you, yes."

"This one's not a simple yes or no." He smiled and reached up to brush a strand of hair behind her ear. "I'd like to take you to dinner. The choice is we can go to a nice place and hope for a quiet evening with no interruptions. Problem is I can't seem to go out into public anymore without someone coming up and wanting to give me their opinion on one thing or another. You need to know that it's a real possibility."

Catie leaned in toward him, enjoying his spicy male scent. "And choice number two?"

"Dinner at my place." His hand slid into her hair and he caressed her scalp. "Just the two of us."

"That's a no brainer." She rose up on her toes and brushed her lips over his. "Let's go to your place."

During the ten mile drive to his ranch, Jarrod had hardly been able to keep his hands or his eyes off Catie. The way her nipples had been poking beneath her top, he'd been able to tell that she wasn't wearing a bra, and he'd almost bet that she didn't have on any panties, either. His cock had hardened to uncomfortable proportions at the thought of touching and tasting that satiny smooth pussy he'd stroked just a couple of nights ago.

Instead of copping a feel, he kept his hands glued to the steering wheel as they'd talked about everything from the weather to what he'd done before he became sheriff. Whenever he tried to steer the conversation around to her, Catie managed to evade his questions. As though she didn't like talking about herself...or maybe she had something to hide?

He pushed the thought to the back of his mind as he guided the truck from the highway, up the short dirt road, and then parked in front of his home.

"Nice," Catie murmured, peering at the house through the starlit night. "What I can see of it, anyway."

Jarrod opened his door and walked around to help Catie, only she was out of the truck before he made it to her side. He took her hand and led her to the house, enjoying the feel of her fingers twined with his.

He unlocked the front door and let her in, then closing it behind them. "How does steak sound?" he asked as he flipped on the track lighting.

"As long as it's medium rare, I'll love it."

"Done." He took off his western hat and tossed it onto the back of a recliner, then raked his fingers through his hair.

Catie slid off her jean jacket and laid it next to his hat as she glanced around the living room that was done in western décor from oxblood brown leather sofas and chairs to end tables made from knotty pine. Bookcases along one wall were filled with novels on the American West, along with tales by Zane Grey and other western authors.

"For a bachelor, you have great taste." She moved to one end table and touched the bronze statue of a bucking bronco doing its best to unseat its rider.

Jarrod's mouth watered as he watched Catie trail her fingers down the statue. He cleared his throat and came to stand beside her. "My youngest sister's into decorating and insisted that a sheriff needs appropriate digs."

"It suits you." Catie tilted her head up and looked at him, her lips slightly parted, her chocolate eyes focused on him. "Rough…untamed…and utterly male." The desire in her gaze slammed into him like a fist to his gut. Before he even had a chance to act on his instinct, she moved into his arms and wrapped her arm around his neck.

"I don't know what you do to me," she murmured. "But all I can think about is sex when I'm near you."

"You make it real hard to think about anything else." Jarrod pulled her body tight against his and fisted his hands under her jean skirt. His fingers slid along her bare ass as he discovered she was wearing nothing underneath, just like the other night. A groan rumbled from his chest, his cock throbbing with scalding need to be buried inside Catie's core.

She reached up and flicked her tongue over his bottom lip and then gently nipped it. Damn but the sensation was erotic. He'd never had a woman bite his lip before, and he couldn't believe how horny it made him — and he'd been beyond horny for her since before the night began.

Unable to stand her sweet torture any longer, Jarrod crushed his mouth against hers, devouring her, filling himself with her sweet taste. Catie's tongue met his, her kiss as hard and demanding as his own.

He raised her skirt to her waist, then grabbed her ass, lifting her up and pressing her bare pussy to his erection. She wrapped her legs around his waist, clamping him tight as her hands clenched in his hair and they ravaged each other's mouth.

Catie couldn't believe how wild she was for this man. She *needed* to feel his naked skin next to hers, to feel his cock sliding into her.

"Fuck me, Jarrod." Her voice was husky as she pulled back and looked into his eyes. "Right here. Right now."

"Damn, Catie." Jarrod moved his lips to her neck and she gasped at the sensual feel of his mustache along her throat. "I've never met a woman like you."

With her legs still wrapped around him, he walked to an overstuffed chair near a fireplace. He set her down, her naked ass on the cool leather of the chair, her skirt hiked up to her waist. As he knelt between her thighs, she kicked off her shoes and spread her legs.

"I want you naked." Catie reached for him, but he captured both her wrists in one of his big hands.

He gave her a sexy grin that sent tingles straight through her belly to her pussy and made her absolutely drenched for him. "I need a little appetizer first." With her wrists held in one of his hands, he held them over her head while pressing closer to her. His masculine scent filled her senses, driving her crazy, making her want him so badly that she wriggled and moaned.

With his free hand, Jarrod reached up and tugged on her strapless top, pulling it down to see her small breasts and pert nipples. "Mmmm. Beautiful," he murmured before lowering his head and licking one of her diamond-hard nubs.

Catie gasped, her back arching up as wild sensations coursed through her body. She struggled to free her hands as Jarrod suckled first one nipple, then the other. His mustache brushed across her sensitized skin and she could swear she was going to come just from the sensation of his mouth, lips and mustache on her breasts. The feel of her skirt and top around her waist, with the leather of the chair against her bared skin was incredible.

"Let me touch you." She clamped her knees around his waist, locking her ankles behind his back and pressing his jean-clad crotch tighter to her pussy.

"You enjoy watching people have sex." He kissed a trail from her breasts to her neck as he spoke. "I'll bet you'd like to be tied up and fucked."

"God, yes." Catie moaned at him saying one of her fantasies aloud, and she knew she couldn't wait another moment to have him inside her. "I can't take anymore."

"Such a wild little thing." Jarrod lowered her arms, but didn't release her wrists. Instead he kept a hold on them as he eased down. She smelled the scent of her juices as he widened her legs further and ran his tongue along the inside of her thighs.

"Dammit, Jarrod!" Catie squirmed, dying for him to lick her clit. To do anything to bring her some relief. She'd never wanted anything as bad as she wanted Jarrod's cock inside her.

"You like it fast and hard, don't you?" His tongue moved closer to her mound. "Slow and easy drives you crazy, doesn't it?"

"Yes, you bastard." Catie clenched her teeth and arched her back up off the chair. "Dammit. Now lick my clit."

Jarrod chuckled, the feel of his warm breath against her skin almost enough to send her over the pinnacle. "I do love a shaved pussy." He ran his tongue up her slit and she cried out from the feel of it. "And you have a gorgeous pussy."

Catie was about to yell at him again when he pressed his mouth tight to her drenched folds. He plunged his finger inside her, thrusting it in and out of her as he licked and sucked on her clit. She fought against his hold on her wrists, wanting to clench her hands in his hair, but at the same time totally turned-on by being held prisoner to his will.

Her climax hit her so hard that she shrieked and clamped her knees tight around his head. "Stop," she begged as aftershock upon aftershock wracked her body. "I can't take anymore."

But Jarrod continued to lick her clit until she reached climax again. And then again.

Chapter Four

Catie was still recovering from that third orgasm when Jarrod released her wrists, scooped her up, and stood. Her world spun and she gasped as she flung her arms around his neck and held on while he strode from the living room.

"Where are you taking me?" she asked as she clung to him.

"My room." His stride was deliberate, his jaw set as he carried her through the large home.

"'Bout time." She caught glimpses of a large stainless-steel kitchen that would make a chef envious, as well as a kitchen nook with a bay window and a formal dining room. The house smelled warm and inviting, a spicy masculine scent that reminded her of Jarrod.

His boots rang against the tile as he headed down a short hall and through double doors into a massive bedroom. Light from the hallway poured through the doors, illuminating the rough-hewn wooden furniture and a king-sized bed smack dab in the middle of the room.

One-handed, he flipped on the lamp on the nightstand beside the bed, and the room filled with a soft amber glow. He set her on the comforter and tugged off her skirt and top before she had a chance to even think straight.

Catie had never thought of herself as beautiful, not like her friend Dee. As far as Catie was concerned, she was too thin with not enough curves, as well as being smallchested. But right now, with the way Jarrod just stood there and looked at her with hunger, desire and admiration in his green eyes, she felt absolutely gorgeous.

She eased off the comforter to stand on the small rug at his bedside as he toed off his boots and yanked off his socks. "Let me undress you," she said.

But when she reached for his shirt, he caught her wrists. "I don't know if I can wait that long."

"Fair's fair." Catie gave him a saucy smile, but inside she was a quivering mass of lust. Every cell in her body screamed with need for this man. Need to have his naked form against hers, need to taste his skin and his come, and need to see if he fit as perfectly inside as he did outside.

Jarrod released her, but a muscle in his cheek twitched and she could tell he was barely able to rein himself in. He clenched and unclenched his fists. "You'd better hurry, woman."

With a soft laugh, Catie grabbed the bottom of his shirt, brought it up to his chest, and he helped her pull it over his head. The action mussed his thick sable hair, giving him an untamed and dangerous look.

"Mmmm." She ran her palms over his muscled chest, enjoying the feel of him. "Now keep your hands to yourself while I get my turn at you." Breathing deeply of his scent, she leaned forward and flicked her tongue against his nipple, and delighted in the way he sucked in his breath. His biceps flexed as he fought for control.

His salty taste rolled over her tongue as she licked a path from one nipple, through the light dusting of hair on his chest, to the other nipple. Her hands continued exploring him, moving to his shoulders and along his arms to his wrists, and then back up and down his chest to his flat belly. She loved the ripple of muscle beneath his smooth skin and the way his taut stomach clenched beneath her touch.

"Dammit, Catie." A growl rumbled up in Jarrod's chest, reverberating through her as she continued kissing and licking him.

"Don't tell me you like it hard and fast." She trailed her tongue in lazy circles down his belly toward his waistband. "I thought you enjoyed slow and easy."

Jarrod thought he was going to climax in his jeans from the way the woman was torturing him. "Honey, when it comes to you, I have a feeling nothing's easy."

"Oh?" She tugged at his belt and pulled it out of the belt loops, her chocolate eyes meeting his. "I sure said yes mighty fast to you in the barn. What do you call that?" Catie placed her hand on his cock and rubbed it through the denim.

His dick throbbed at her touch. "There's a difference between going after what you want and being easy."

"I like the way you think, cowboy." With nimble fingers she unfastened his jeans, tugged them down, and gasped when his cock sprang out. "Damn. I knew you were big, but...damn."

When she looked up at him, he raised an eyebrow at her wide-eyed expression.

A mischievous light sparked in her eyes. "In case you're wondering, that's a good thing."

He grinned as she pulled his jeans and briefs down past his hips and he stepped out of them. "Thank god for small favors."

Catie knelt on the rug at his feet and wrapped her fingers around his cock. Her hair shimmered gold in the lamp's glow as she shook her head. "In your case, I'd say it was a rather large favor." Before he had a chance to respond, she swirled her tongue over the head of his cock.

Jarrod's hips bucked and he slid his hands into her hair, unable to keep from touching her any longer. He could barely remember to breathe as he watched her lips slide down his cock, taking him deep. Her mouth felt warm and wet, and better than he had imagined. And he had imagined plenty since meeting Catie.

Her eyes met his as she continued easing her lips up and down his cock. She moved one hand to his balls, gently playing with them while her other hand worked his staff in time with the motion of her mouth.

He clenched his fingers in her silken strands and gritted his teeth. "You're going to be swallowing my come real fast if you don't slow down."

In response she hummed, the vibration burning through his cock like a match-lit fuse. His balls drew up and his groin tightened as the sensation shoved him over the edge and straight into an explosive orgasm.

Jarrod's hands tightened in Catie's hair as come shot from his cock and into her mouth. She never let up, not for a moment, continuing to suck on him until she'd swallowed it all. She would have kept going, but he managed to use his strength to his advantage and disengaged his wet member from her mouth.

His breathing came hard, sweat cooling his skin, as he braced his hands on her shoulders. Catie grinned up at him, licking her lips like a cat cleaning the last bit of cream from her whiskers.

"Remind me not to piss you off," Jarrod murmured as he gripped her shoulders and drew her up to him. "You know how to get your revenge, don't you?"

Sliding her hands around his neck, she melded her lithe body against his. "Are you complaining?"

He chuckled and pressed his lips to her forehead. "Not on your life."

Satisfaction warmed Catie's belly, knowing that she'd given him as much pleasure as he'd given her. A smile curved her lips as she nuzzled his chest. "You need time to regenerate, or are you ready to fuck me?"

Jarrod growled as he grabbed her ass and pressed his thick erection to her belly. "What do you think?"

"Oooh, you're hard again." She stood up on her toes and brushed her mouth over his, loving the way his mustache felt against her lips. "So what are you waiting for?"

He clasped his big hands around her slim waist and practically tossed her on the bed. Catie laughed and brushed her hair out of her eyes. But her laughter faded as she saw the look on Jarrod's face—like he was up to no good.

His mustache twitched as he reached over to the dresser and grabbed something off the top, and Catie caught the glint of metal.

She furrowed her brow as he moved onto the bed and knelt between her thighs. "What are you up to?" she asked as she tried to see what he was holding, but he held it behind his back.

Jarrod put his free hand by her head and captured her gaze with his. "So...you've fantasized about being tied up, have you?"

Warmth crept through Catie, but it wasn't because she was embarrassed at having so easily admitted her fantasy. It was more the way he looked at her—like he intended to do something about it.

"Yeah…" No sooner had she said the word, than Jarrod brought the hand out that he'd been hiding and clamped cold steel around her wrist. "Hey—" she started, but he moved so fast that the next thing she knew he had her arms stretched over her head. He flipped the free cuff over the railing behind her, and then clasped the cuff to her other wrist.

"Oh, my god." Catie twisted as she pulled against the cuffs, the metal slightly digging into her flesh. Her pussy flooded with moist heat at the feel of being handcuffed and completely vulnerable to the man between her thighs. "I can't believe you really did it."

"Change your mind?" Jarrod pressed his cock to her belly, his gaze like green fire licking through her body.

"No way." Tingles skittered through Catie's belly and her nipples tightened. "And in case you're wondering, I've had all my tests, I'm clean, *and* I'm on the pill. What about you, cowboy?"

"Clean bill of health all the way around." He gave her his sexy smile. "Shall I get out my donor card?"

"Anybody else, yes. You, I trust." She wrapped her legs around his waist. "So fuck me, dammit."

His mouth came down on hers, crushing her lips, as though punishing her for making him desire her so much. Even though she knew it was fruitless, she pulled against the cuffs, wanting to reach around him and dig her nails into his back.

Jarrod hooked his arms under her knees and raised her up, opening her wide to him. He released one knee long enough to guide his cock toward her slick opening. "Am I too big for you?"

"Never." She strained against the cuffs, arching her back. "Now, Jarrod!"

Catie gasped as he slid the head of his cock into her opening, stretching her with his thickness. He grabbed both of her ankles and moved them up to his neck, so that her feet were to either side of his head, and she could feel the softness of his hair along her instep. His eyes focused on hers, his breathing hard as he eased himself in another inch and then paused.

She raised her hips up, taking him deeper. "Give me all of you and stop messing with me."

The irritating man just grabbed her hips and gave her another fraction of his cock. "We have all night, honey."

Narrowing her eyes, Catie did her best to glare at him. "You'd better fuck me now, or there'll be hell to pay later."

Jarrod grinned. "All right, little wildcat. You want a fucking, a fucking's what you're gonna get."

He thrust his cock into her, burying himself within her pussy. Catie cried out at the sensation of having him so deep inside, stretching her and filling her completely.

"You okay?" Jarrod held still, sweat beading on his forehead and trickling down the side of his face.

"Oh, yeah." Catie wiggled, enjoying the incredible fullness of his cock inside her. "I'll be even better once you get to it."

With slow, even thrusts, he began moving within her core, holding her ass while he rose up on his knees. "You feel so good," he murmured.

She glanced down to where they were joined, mesmerized by the sight of his cock moving in and out of her pussy. He was so big and thick, and it felt incredible. She had never been able to come without her clit being stimulated, but to her amazement, she already felt an orgasm coming on.

His pace increased, his flesh slapping against hers. "I love the way you watch me while I'm fucking you."

Her gaze moved to his and her stomach flipped at the look in his eyes. "Harder." Straining against the handcuffs, she tried to buck her hips. "I'm almost there."

Jarrod released her ass and reached around her legs to tweak her nipples, and at the same time began pounding into her like she wanted him to.

"Yeah...just like that." A faint buzzing started in Catie's ears as he drove into her. The noise grew to a dull roar. Her stomach muscles clenched and her core contracted, gripping Jarrod tighter.

"Come on, honey." His voice was hoarse, like he could barely hold himself back from climaxing.

"Oh...my...*god*." Catie's entire being vibrated as she grew closer and closer to the peak. "Don't stop, Jarrod. Fuck me even harder."

He growled, his balls slapping her ass as he pistoned his hips against hers.

"Yes!" she screamed as she came, her body jerking with the force of each wave of her orgasm.

Jarrod continued driving his cock into her core, drawing along each undulation.

"Catie. Oh, damn," he called out as he reached his climax, his hot semen squirting inside her. His cock was so large she felt every throb and pulse of his orgasm. He moved within her, slower and slower until he finally stopped, his hips fused against hers.

After a moment, he eased her legs down from around his neck so that her feet were resting on the comforter, his cock still buried in her pussy. His weight felt comfortable as he relaxed on top of her, his stubble-roughened cheek resting next to hers. Smells of sex and sweat sifted through the air and Catie sighed, more sated and content than she could remember feeling before.

"Mmmmm, Jarrod?" She moved her cheek against his, enjoying his stubble scraping her soft skin. "I hate to break this moment, but you think you could unlock these handcuffs?"

"I don't know." He propped himself up on both arms and his lips quirked in a grin. "Kinda like you right where I've got you."

"Oh?" Damn but he made her feel all quivery and gooey inside. "What do I have to do to convince you?"

Jarrod raised an eyebrow. "Of what?"

"That there'll be hell to pay if you don't get these things off me now."

With a soft laugh he rolled off of her, his cock sliding out of her pussy and making her feel empty without him. He was still semi-erect and glistening with her juices as he went to the dresser and rummaged through the top drawer. "Now supposing I can't find the key?"

Catie glared at him. "Supposing I'm gonna kick your ass, cowboy."

Keys jangled as he returned. He held them in his palm, a wicked look in his green eyes. "How about we strike a deal?"

"Jarrod…" She swallowed back her retort as his gaze swept over her naked form from her arms stretched over her head, on down, settling on her shaved mound. While he studied her his cock lengthened, and her mouth watered to taste him again. He looked magnificent, his body so muscular and sculpted. Catie's nipples hardened and her core flooded as he smiled and met her eyes.

He sat on the edge of the bed, and brushed his lips over hers. "I'll let you go if you promise to stay the night."

Catie stilled and her heart pounded out a strange cadence in her throat. "I don't stay the night with anyone." It was one thing to enjoy sex, it was another to wake up with a man and have breakfast with him.

"Stay with me." His words were a demand, definitely not a request.

She shook her head, but when she spoke, the word barely came out in a whisper. "No."

"That's my condition, little wildcat." Jarrod pressed his forehead to hers. "I aim to tame you."

Chapter Five

The man was serious—Catie could see it in Jarrod's eyes, could hear it in his tone. Yet at the same time she couldn't believe he intended to keep her cuffed to the bed until she agreed to spend the night with him.

"What'll it be, honey?" Jarrod brushed his lips over hers, and sparks skittered through her belly like a dozen firecrackers. "I'll feed you in bed if you'd rather be cuffed all night."

All right. *Fine.* If he wanted to play rough, she'd give him as good as he dished out.

Like hell he would tame her. And before sunrise she *would* get her own revenge.

When he drew back, Catie glared at him the best she could manage. "I'll spend the night, but only because I don't particularly feel like being cuffed to the bed."

A smug smile crossed Jarrod's handsome features as he reached up, removed the cuffs and tossed them on the comforter. He massaged her wrists, the sensation of his touch soothing and arousing all at once. Passion burned through Catie, coupled with warmth from the caring she witnessed in his expression.

Even though she barely knew him, somehow this man stirred emotions and longings within her that she didn't want to admit, and had never allowed herself to consider.

Like a possibility of happiness and a future with one man.

No, dammit. Make believe and fairy tales—she didn't believe in either.

Jarrod pressed his lips to the inside of one of her wrists, and flicked his tongue against her pulse point, sending a shiver throughout her body. "You ready for some chow?" he murmured.

"S-sure." She frowned at the way her voice trembled. What the hell was he doing to her?

Satisfaction curled in Jarrod's gut as he took her by the hand and helped her off the bed. He'd always been able to trust his instinct, and that instinct had told him from the beginning that Catie shied away from real intimacy. Why she was afraid of a serious relationship, he didn't know, but he was determined to find out.

And by the time all was said and done, she'd be his.

Catie took her hand from his grasp and scooped his shirt from the floor. Her voice was muffled as she pulled it over her head. "So what's for dinner, other than steak?"

When she reappeared, static caused her hair to poke up all over her in a blonde halo. She was so petite that his shirt reached her knees, and she looked like a woodland pixie. Jarrod grinned, holding back a laugh.

"What?" Catie put her hands on her slim hips and narrowed her gaze.

"You." Shaking his head, he took her by the shoulders and kissed her forehead, then drew back to look at her again. "You're adorable."

"Hmph." She tried to look grouchy, but in his gut Jarrod knew it was all an act. For some reason she preferred to keep an emotional distance, which was something he'd have to change.

He released her shoulders to grab his briefs and jeans off the floor, then pulled them on. "How about rolls, tossed salad and mashed potatoes? I might even be able to come up with something for dessert, too."

"I have to warn you, I'm not into cooking, so I won't be much help." Catie walked at his side as he headed out of the bedroom toward the kitchen. "If it wasn't for pre-packaged meals and the microwave, Steve and I would probably starve."

At the mention of her brother, a cloud passed through Jarrod's consciousness. It probably wasn't real smart of him to fuck a suspect's sister, but when it came to Catie, Jarrod had to make an exception.

"Dinner's my treat, so sit your pretty ass down," he said as they reached the kitchen. He took a package of t-bones out of the fridge and brought them to the grill built into the center of the stovetop. "My mom saw to it that my sisters and I learned how to cook."

"Ooooh, a man who's great in bed *and* knows how to whip up a meal." Catie moved to the breakfast bar and eased up onto a stool. "If you clean, too, I think I've struck pay dirt."

Jarrod grinned as he turned on the grill, then grabbed a stoneware plate out of the cabinet. "I have a housekeeper who comes in a couple of times a week."

"Even better." Mischief sparked in Catie's eyes. "Leaves more time for all that great sex."

His gaze met hers. "Better watch it, honey, or dinner'll be late."

"Promises, promises." Her voice was teasing, but her nipples poked through his shirt. He had no doubt she'd love it if he fucked her right there in the kitchen.

She cleared her throat. "So...you actually like to cook?"

With effort, Jarrod reined in his lust and took the steaks out of the package. "I have nothing against going out for a meal or heating up something in the microwave." He slapped the steaks onto the stoneware plate and seasoned them liberally with salt and pepper. "But sometimes I find it kinda relaxing to cook up a good meal, like Mom makes."

Catie enjoyed watching Jarrod as he fixed their dinner. The man was powerful and sensual, in command of his environment no matter where he was. Even in the kitchen.

He looked so damn sexy in only his jeans, his chest bare and hair mussed. Her palms itched to touch him again, and she couldn't wait to breathe deep of his masculine scent, or to feel his cock plunging inside her pussy. She grew wetter by the moment as she remembered how it had felt to have him inside her core, and her ankles up around his neck.

For awhile she was silent while she studied him, his muscles rippling in the soft lighting. With efficient movements he cut up potatoes and placed them in a pot with water to boil, then started putting together a salad with fixings he grabbed from the fridge.

Cocking her head to the side, she asked, "I've been wondering what you were doing on my ranch that night we, ah, met."

The corner of his mouth quirked into a smile as he chopped a tomato on a cutting board. "When you were being a Peeping Tomasina?"

"Peeping Tomasina, huh?" A giggle escaped her before she could stop it. "Don't tell me you were being Tom."

"Not intentionally." He tossed the tomatoes into a bowl with lettuce greens. "I was out doing investigative work. Trying to see if I could come up with some leads on those damn rustlers."

"Ah." Catie propped her elbow on the breakfast bar as she watched him, her chin resting in her hand. "So, tell me about your family. Like how many sisters you have."

"Three." Jarrod gave her a quick grin as he tossed the steaks onto the grill. "I'm the oldest. I think that's what got me interested in law enforcement—I was always on the lookout for those girls. They were bound and determined to get into as much trouble as possible, and I was determined to keep them out of it."

"Uh-huh. An overprotective older brother." Catie smiled at the thought of Jarrod chasing off his sisters' boyfriends. "I have one of those. Steve made it known that if any guys messed with me, he'd kick their asses." She shook her head and rolled her eyes. "Needless to say, it was not real good for my social life, considering Steve was one of the buffest jocks in school." Of course he'd done saved her ass once, too.

Was it her imagination, or did Jarrod's eyes narrow at the mention of her brother's name?

But Jarrod just nodded and gave her a quick grin. "I bet he had to kick a lot of ass to keep the guys away from you."

"Yeah, right." Catie snorted. "I didn't develop as fast as most girls, so I was more like one of the guys. At least until I was a junior and my boobs actually decided to grow, even if it was just a little bit."

Jarrod's eyes shot from the steaks to Catie. "You're perfect." He set down the fork he'd been holding, and in just a couple of steps, he was at her side. She caught her breath as he lifted the shirt she was wearing and captured her breasts in his hands. "Pert, beautiful nipples. And more than a mouthful."

He ducked his head and suckled one of her hard nubs. Catie gasped as he flicked his tongue over her nipple, then gently pulled at it with his teeth, before moving to the other breast. Her pussy flooded with moisture and she squirmed at the feel of him licking and sucking her nipples.

In the background she could hear the sizzle of the steaks on the grill and the hiss of water on the stovetop as the potatoes boiled over. But Jarrod didn't seem to care. His thumb found her clit and he thrust his fingers into her core.

Catie slid her hands into his hair and held on, lost in the feelings he stirred within her. A moan escaped her lips as he sucked and gently bit at each nipple while his thumb teased her clit, his fingers still deep inside her pussy.

The orgasm flamed through her body, and she cried out from the searing pleasure of her release. Her hips jerked against Jarrod's hand as he continued to move his fingers in and out.

"Stop." She put her hands on his shoulders, her body throbbing. "No more."

Jarrod eased his fingers from her core and raised his head. His eyes fixed on her and he licked his fingers. Every slow stroke of his tongue was like he was licking her pussy, tasting her. Even though he was no longer touching her, it felt like he was, and she couldn't stop trembling from her climax.

"Damn you taste good." He brushed his mouth over hers, his mustache tickling her lips, the warmth of his breath adding heat to her blood. "I'd better see to dinner before something burns," he murmured, then turned back to the stove.

Too late, the thought went through Catie's fuzzy mind. She was burning all over.

After they'd eaten a bowl of chocolate fudge ice cream for dessert, Jarrod took Catie on a tour of his ranch style home. He enjoyed showing it to her, and how she seemed to appreciate the custom-built house. He'd had it built only a year prior, and it was his sanctuary away from the demands of his job and the political aspects of being the county sheriff.

They ended up in his den, where he worked at home from time to time. He flicked on the track lighting which illuminated glossy oak furnishings and floor-to-ceiling shelves lining two walls. Books on Arizona, Native American, U.S., and world history lined the shelves, along with professional journals and handbooks, biographies and anything else that had caught his interest. Navajo artwork that he'd collected over the years covered the walls as well as dotting the shelves, along with pictures of his family. The room smelled of books, lemon oil polish, and of the case of cherry pipe tobacco that he kept to remind him of his dad.

From off the oak credenza, Catie picked up a carved wooden caricature of an old cowboy with a drooping mustache and a ten-gallon hat that looked like it had a hole shot through the top of the crown. "This is great. Who's the artist?"

"I am." Jarrod smiled when her gaze cut to his, her eyes wide. "Wood carving is a hobby of mine. I have a little workshop in the back of the house."

Wrinkling her nose, she placed the cowboy back on the shelf. "That's disgusting."

He raised a brow. "You don't like it?"

"Love it." Catie poked his chest with one finger. "What's disgusting is that you're not only a good fuck, know how to cook, have great taste in decorating and are well read, but you're artistic too."

His mouth curved into a grin. "Don't forget kind to animals and small children."

"So I see." She walked away from him to the shelves and ran her fingers along one of the framed photographs. "Whose kids?"

"Between two of my three sisters, I have six nieces and nephews. That's Brian, the youngest of the bunch. They're good kids." Jarrod eased behind Catie, gripped her shoulders and nuzzled her neck. "Do you want to have rug rats of your own one day?"

A tingling sensation sparked in her belly, but she refused to dwell on it. Instead she shrugged and moved her hand away from the picture. "I don't plan on ever getting married, so likely not."

Jarrod turned her around and moved her so that her butt was backed up to the massive oak desk. "What's spooked you?" He hooked his forefinger under her chin and raised it so that her eyes met his. "Why are you afraid of getting serious about anyone?"

"Because relationships never last." Catie's gaze was defiant, but her hand went to her earlobe and she tugged on the gold earring. "I wouldn't put any kid through what I grew up with."

With a gentle hand, he swept a strand of blonde hair from her face. "And what's that?"

"Being torn between parents who hate each other while they play tug of war with you." Her jaw hardened and she pulled harder at her ear. "Having your mom take off with some man and never seeing her again because she'd rather fuck than be around her own kids. Watching your dad marry and divorce so many times you can't remember the names of all your stepparents or stepbrothers and sisters."

He brushed his knuckles along her cheek to her ear and captured her hand in his, pulling it away from her lobe. "Honey, just because they didn't know how to make a relationship work doesn't mean you'll follow in their footsteps." Jarrod released her to let his hands slide down to her waist then drew her closer. "You're not your parents."

Catie could hardly think with his cock pressed against her belly. Now was not the time to think about her history, or her future. She wanted him again, and she wanted him *now*. Bracing her hands on the desk behind her, she widened her stance. "Shut up and fuck me."

Jarrod's green eyes flared. In a quick movement that left her breathless, he raised her up and placed her on the desk, its polished surface cool beneath her bare ass. He yanked the shirt over her head and tossed it on the floor, then unfastened his jeans and shoved them with his briefs down his hips, releasing his cock.

She spread her thighs and he guided his cock into her dripping core in one quick thrust. Pure pleasure rippled through Catie at the feel of him inside her, and she wrapped her legs around his waist. She flattened her hands on the desktop and tilted her head back, lost in the sensations.

"Watch." Jarrod's voice was gruff as he grasped her thighs with his hands. "Watch me fuck you."

Catie looked down at where they were joined. The mere sight of his cock thrusting in and out of her pussy was enough to drive her closer and closer to peak. Her juices coated him, his length glistening in the low den lighting.

Lowering his head, he pressed his mouth against hers, urging her up to meet him. His tongue slid between her lips, matching the motion and rhythm of his cock.

She moaned into his mouth, dizzy, wild with lust. The smell of their sex was an aphrodisiac, heightening her arousal, sending her senses spiraling. Her body was hot, her nipples tingling with every brush of his solid chest.

He raised his head and glanced to where his cock moved within her pussy, then back to her eyes. "You fit me perfectly, Catie Wilds." He drove into her, harder and harder yet.

She gasped and her eyes widened as her body trembled with the oncoming climax

"That's it." Jarrod gripped her legs tighter, never slowing in his motion. "Come on, honey."

Catie cried out as the muscles in her belly contracted with each wave of her orgasm. Every thrust of his cock sent another swell of pleasure throughout her body. It seemed like her climax would never end. Like she'd be locked with him forever, her body shuddering with every crest and ebb.

Even as he shouted her name, even as his cock jerked and throbbed within her core, Catie was swept away in a tidal wave of sensation that threatened to drown her.

Threatened to steal her heart and never let go.

* * * * *

The telephone's incessant ring broke into Jarrod's climax-fogged mind. If it didn't mean pulling his cock from Catie's warm depths, he would have reached over and thrown that damn telephone out the window.

"You're in hot demand, Sheriff." Catie's teasing voice murmured in his ear as the answering machine clicked on and she heard a standard message being played. "You gonna get that?"

"No." The word was a rumble in Jarrod's chest as he kissed the soft skin of her neck. "Whoever it is can go to hell for all I care."

The outgoing message stopped, and then Deputy Forrester came on the line. "Sheriff, I need a word with you. It's about St—"

The moment he heard Forrester's voice, Jarrod moved so fast that he was able to pick up the phone just as the man said, "Wilds."

"I'm right here," Jarrod growled, yanking up his jeans and looking away from Catie's frown. "What's so damn important that you had to call me at home on my day off?"

"Uh, well…" The deputy sounded like he was uncomfortable with the news he was relaying. "Kev Grand said he was out checking his fence line the other night. The same night someone tried to mess with that new bull of the MacLeod's. Claims he saw a horse and rider leaving the Flying M Ranch—and he recognized the horse."

Jarrod's gaze flicked to Catie. She was still naked, but now looking at the carvings of old cowpokes that he'd done. "And…" he prompted Forrester.

"Grand says it was Catie Wilds' appaloosa, and the rider was the same size as Steve."

"Shit." Jarrod drew in a harsh breath and Catie's gaze shot to him. She bit her lower lip and scooped the T-shirt off the floor and left his den, probably to give him some privacy.

"What do you want me to do, Sheriff?" Forrester asked in an even tone.

"Nothing yet. Let me check things out." Jarrod stared out the door Catie had disappeared through. "You just see what else you can dig up. And don't narrow the focus. Got me?"

After he hung up with Forrester, Jarrod stroked his hand over his mustache, trying to puzzle through what was going on. Steve Wilds had motive and opportunity, but did he have the connections to rustle all the cattle, then liquidate them for cash?

Although the evidence was starting to point at Wilds, something in Jarrod's gut told him it was all too neat. There was a hell of a lot going on around here—more than what met the eye.

He picked up the receiver and dialed up Rocky Brogan, a buddy of his that could do some quick, efficient research—beyond anything he could manage to scrape together through the Sheriff's Department.

"Brogan here," the man's baritone came on the line.

"Jarrod Savage." His eyes remained on the doorway, making sure Catie didn't come marching through, and he kept his voice low. "I need you to get some down and dirty on a few characters."

"Shoot, pardner."

"All currently reside in or around Douglas, Arizona." Clearing his throat, Jarrod continued, "Steve Wilds, part owner of the Wilds Ranch. Jake Reynolds, Intelligence Agent with Customs, just married the owner of the Flying M, or so my big-mouthed secretary claims. Jess Lawless, foreman for the Flying M. Kev Grand, owner of the Bar One." Jarrod's brow furrowed as he gave the last name. "And Ryan Forrester, Cochise County Deputy."

Brogan repeated all the information and punctuated it with a small grunt. "Give me a couple of days."

"Thanks," Jarrod replied. "I'll look for it Monday."

After he placed the receiver back on the cradle, Jarrod rubbed his forehead, trying to ease the beginnings of a headache. Damn but he didn't like the way things were turning. Didn't like it at all.

Chapter Six

Golden light of a new morning spilled through the shutters and onto Jarrod's eyelids, but he was too comfortable holding his little wildcat. He kept his eyes closed, enjoying the feel of her in his arms, filling his lungs with her perfume of vanilla musk and the scents of their mingled sex.

Catie stirred next to him, her hip rubbing against his hard-as-iron cock. "Better watch it," he murmured, his voice thick with sleep. "Or I might just have to wake you properly."

"Oh, yeah?" Her tone was light and teasing as she caressed his forearm.

But then he heard a familiar metal click at the same moment cool metal clamped around his wrist.

His eyes shot open and he yanked his arm, only to have metal dig into his flesh. He was handcuffed to the bedrail.

Catie giggled, rolling away from him and off the bed before he had the chance to grab her with his free hand. She dragged the comforter along with her so that he was completely naked, then dropped it to the floor as she said, "I told you that you'd pay."

"You sure did." Jarrod couldn't help but grin at the sight of her eyes glinting with laughter. But his smile faded as his gaze traveled down her length, from her tousled hair to her pert nipples, on past her flat stomach to her beautiful shaved mound.

His cock was so hard he was afraid he'd come right on the bed. "Over here. Now."

Her grin widened. "Don't you know? Paybacks are a bitch, sugar."

Letting her gaze linger on his cock, she licked her lips. Something told Jarrod he just might enjoy her version of paybacks. But then again, when it came to Catie Wilds, nothing was a certainty. And nothing was easy.

"I have to teach you a lesson." She walked around the bed, studying him like a buyer examining a bull at an auction. "Now I could just leave you locked up—take your truck and go on home."

Jarrod frowned. "Uh, honey—"

"Hold on, I'm thinking here." Catie held up her hand, a look of serious consideration on her face. "Or I could force you to have wild sex with me."

"That'd be a hardship." Jarrod's cock jumped against his belly, and he held back a grin. "But I think I could manage."

"Hmmm." She strolled closer to his side of the bed, but kept her enticing body out of reach. "Of course, I could always get my revenge in another way."

A rumble of sheer lust rose up in his throat, and he bit the inside of his cheek so hard he tasted blood.

"Do you want to touch me, Jarrod?" Slowly, deliberately, she ran her tongue along her lower lip while she cupped her breasts in her palms, her chocolate eyes focused on him.

"Yeah." His voice was hoarse and he swallowed, hard, then swallowed again as she pulled at her pert nipples. Nipples he wanted to suck and lick and nip at with his teeth.

A sensual smile teased the corner of her mouth as she let one of her hands drift down her flat belly to her silken mound. "Would you like to see me touch myself?"

"Catie…" Jarrod groaned and pulled against the restraint, wondering if he could bust the rail, snatch her before she knew he was loose, and fuck her ten ways 'til Sunday. His cock was so hard it practically pointed toward the ceiling.

"How about if I make myself come while you watch?" She widened her stance and slipped her fingers into her pussy. Her lips parted and her eyelids fluttered as she stroked her clit with one hand while tweaking her nipple with her other. "I like how you fuck me, Jarrod." Again she licked her lips, this time her gaze focused on his cock. "Would you like to fuck me now?"

"Hell, yes." The cuff rattled against the rail as he strained against it.

"What if I sit on your face?" Catie seemed lost in the sensations of taunting him while stroking her pussy herself. "Would you like that?"

He clenched his fist and practically growled at her. "Why don't I show you?"

She turned her back to him and bent over, her legs parted so that he could clearly see her beautiful shaved pussy, and her fingers teasing her clit. Looking over her shoulder, she said, "Would you like to fuck me from behind?"

Jarrod roared and slid his legs over the side of the bed, trying to grab her with his free hand. The cuffs slid along the rail, and held fast, keeping Jarrod only inches from reaching Catie.

She taunted him as she looked over her shoulder and gave him that sexy smile. "Yeah, that's it."

He yanked so hard against the restraints that the bed moved a good six inches.

Catie gasped as Jarrod hooked his free arm around her waist and pulled her ass tight against his throbbing cock. "You need to be punished, woman."

"I have been a bad girl." She bent even lower, rubbing her ass against him. "So what are you going to do about it?"

"I'm going to fuck you until you can't walk straight." Jarrod stepped back against the bed, dragging Catie with him. In a quick motion, he flipped her around. She squealed as she found herself sprawled on the bed, her ass sticking up in the air. It was a tricky maneuver, considering he was handcuffed to the rail, and it didn't leave a lot of room for error. But he was a man bent on fucking his woman.

He guided his cock into her wet folds, nudging her legs farther apart. The walls of her core gripped him tight and he damn near came right then and there.

She moaned as he sank deep inside her pussy. Gripping the bed sheet in her hands, she pressed her ass back against him. "I've been a *real* bad girl. I think you'd better take that into consideration."

The cuff yanked against Jarrod's wrist as he powered his cock within Catie's slick depths. Her passionate cries added even more fuel to his frenzied thrusts.

He didn't have much more time before he came. This woman drove him crazy, made him so damn hot with lust he couldn't think straight. As he pumped in and out of her pussy, he reached around her hips and stroked her clit.

That was all it took. She screamed into the bed sheet, her body tensing against him, the muscles of her core clenching his cock. Jarrod bit back a shout as he came. His dick throbbed and pulsed as he collapsed against her backside, doing his best to keep his weight off her.

"Mmmm." Catie sighed, enjoying the feel of Jarrod's muscled body pressed along her length. She wiggled her hips and was rewarded by the feel of his cock hardening inside her. "What's for breakfast?"

Jarrod chuckled and pressed his lips to her hair. "Depends on whether or not you unlock this cuff."

"And if I say no?"

"Then I keep you right here where I've got you."

"That's not so bad." She shimmied her hips again. "I kinda like it."

"Uh-huh." The cuff rattled against the bedpost as he shifted. "I'm getting a cramp here."

"Ahhh, poor baby." Catie tried to move out from under Jarrod's weight, but he had her pinned tight to the mattress. "Okay. Let me go and I'll get the key."

"How do I know I can trust you?" Jarrod withdrew his cock from her core and eased his weight to the side, but still kept his free arm around her waist. "After all, you are a real bad girl."

"Well,3 next time you can spank me." Her remark was flippant, but in the next second Jarrod smacked her ass with the flat of his hand. "Ow!" Surprise shot through Catie. His hand was so large compared to her butt that both cheeks stung, yet at the same time her pussy flooded with moisture.

"If you're bad, that's what you can expect." He nuzzled her nape, his breath warm across her shoulder blades.

Catie moaned. "Don't forget. This bad girl always gets her revenge."

"I'm counting on it, little wildcat." Low laughter rumbled through Jarrod's chest. "I'm counting on it."

* * * * *

Jarrod asked Catie to spend all of Sunday with him, but she insisted she had to get home and take care of her share of chores around the ranch. He had a feeling, though, that it had more to do with her fear of getting too close to him. Even after all that they had shared since last night, he could sense her pulling away from him, trying to distance her emotions and her heart.

After a leisurely breakfast, Jarrod drove Catie back to her ranch, and then walked her up to the front porch. She paused, her fingers gripping the handle of the screen door, and raised her eyes to meet his. "Thanks for the hot time, cowboy." Her tone was light, but her eyes were so dark they were almost black—like she wanted him right this minute.

"I'm working this area for awhile." He reached up and caught a wisp of her blonde hair, fingering the soft strands. "How 'bout I take you out for dinner tomorrow night. I know a great Mexican restaurant."

She shivered, as though unnerved by his nearness. "I thought you were worried about being mobbed in public."

"It's not so bad early in the week." He moved in closer, pressing her up against the screen. "It's easier to tell a few people to go to hell, rather than a large crowd."

"I...I'm busy Monday." Catie swallowed, her throat working. She put her palms against Jarrod's chest, like she was trying to bolster her determination. "Actually, the whole week's pretty tight."

"Sure it is." He brushed his lips across her forehead, breathing in her vanilla musk scent. Even though they'd taken a shower together, he thought he could still smell the scent of their sex, her juices and his come mingling together. "Change your plans."

"Can't." Her response was barely a whisper as his mouth trailed from her forehead to her ear. She clenched her hands in his shirt and tilted her head back, a soft moan rising in her throat.

"My dad always taught me there's no such word as can't." Jarrod moved his lips over hers. "Anything you truly want, you can have. Anything you put your mind to, you can do."

"And you put your mind to taking me out?" Her breath was warm against his mouth, her gaze focused on his lips.

"Uh-huh." Jarrod took possession of Catie's mouth, his hands sliding around her slender waist and drawing her tight along his length. His cock was hot, throbbing with need again, even after having fucked her so many times. The woman was fire in his blood, singeing him, until she'd burned a permanent hole in his heart. No way was she getting away from him, no matter what she might think.

Her fingers gripped his shirt tighter as their mouths mated. His tongue gained entrance to her willing mouth, and her sweet taste swept through him like the warm rush of rain in a summer thunderstorm.

"Where the hell have you been?" A man's voice growled from the other side of the screen door.

The sound of her brother's voice startled Catie. She jerked her head back, breaking the kiss, but Jarrod held onto her, keeping her pinned to him.

"Dammit, don't sneak up on me like that, Steve." Her tone was slightly breathless as she turned to look at her brother through the screen door.

She glanced back up at Jarrod and saw a predatory look in his eyes. "'Morning, Wilds," Jarrod said as he pulled her away from the door, giving Steve enough room to open it and step through.

Steve glared at Jarrod, that 'protective older brother' look in his brown eyes, then turned his frown on Catie. "Since when do you stay out all night without calling home?"

"You knew where I was." Catie straightened to her full five-feet-four-inches and raised her chin. "I'm twenty-eight years old. I certainly don't need to report in to you."

"Well how about a bit of common courtesy?" He brushed past her and Jarrod and headed to the far end of the porch where an enormous box stood that she hadn't noticed before. "You had me worried."

"You could have called." She pushed away from Jarrod, and felt relieved when he let her go. "What's that?"

Steve dug in his front pocket and pulled out his pocketknife. "New water heater."

"We can't afford that." Catie put her hands on her hips and frowned at her brother. "How in the hell did you pay for it?"

He shrugged and used his knife to slice the plastic straps around the cardboard. "Don't worry. It's taken care of."

"What do you mean, don't worry?" If there was one thing Catie couldn't stand, it was to be told to butt out of something she considered to be her business.

"I said, don't worry about it." Steve spoke through clenched teeth and gave her 'the look' that said they'd discuss it when they didn't have company.

Her gaze shot to Jarrod. He had his thumbs hooked through his belt loops and was watching Steve cut open the box. "Need some help getting that inside the house?" Jarrod asked.

"Sure." Steve gave a quick nod. "If you have the time."

"I've got all day." Jarrod winked at Catie. "I can help you install it if you'd like. I've got some experience there."

Catie raised her hands in exasperation. Here she thought she'd be escaping his incredible masculine magnetism, at least for the rest of the day. Sure, the sex was great, but she needed time to gather her wits. Needed space away from this man who turned her inside out and made her feel like a simpering little fool.

"All right." She moved to the screen door and propped it open. "You two *men* enjoy tearing up the place. Just don't expect me to serve anything fancier than a pitcher of iced tea and a box of macaroni and cheese."

Jarrod flashed her a quick grin. "I like mine extra cheesy."

"I'd like lemon, but no sugar in my tea, Cat," Steve called out as he ripped the cardboard away from the new water heater.

Shaking her head, Catie headed into the house and let the screen door slam behind her.

Men.

Chapter Seven

It was late Monday afternoon by the time Jarrod drove his truck to the Sheriff's office. It had been a tough day all the way around.

Considering he hadn't been able to convince Catie to go out with him during the week, Jarrod was in a pisser of a mood. How the hell was he supposed to wait until Friday to feel her, to taste her, to slide into her heat? His cock throbbed as he guided his truck into his designated parking spot, and he clenched his jaw as he threw the vehicle into park, got out, and headed into the building that housed his office.

He'd spent Sunday helping Steve Wilds put in the heater and had hoped for more time alone with Catie, but she'd managed to thwart him at every turn. Finally he'd told her he'd be there Friday night and would pick her up at seven, end of story.

Apparently it was going to take some work to tame his little wildcat.

Jarrod only nodded to the receptionist as he passed her, then shut the door to his office a little too hard before settling in at his desk. Brogan's info was due—and sure enough, he found Rocky's e-mails the minute he signed on. Frowning, Jarrod went through the facts on each suspect, one by one.

First up was Jake Reynolds, who wasn't really a suspect in Jarrod's mind, but Jarrod had spent too many years on the lines not to consider all his options. Reynolds had a virtually sterling record, first as a sheriff's deputy and then as an agent with Customs for the past decade. The only tarnish on the man's otherwise shiny profile was a drug deal that went bad while he was with Customs. Reynolds had been seriously wounded and ended up in the hospital for a good month, and the perp got away with the dope. IA had performed a thorough investigation, but Reynolds had come up clean.

His frown deepening, Jarrod continued on down to the next name.

Kev Grand had several tickets for speeding and had been thrown in the Douglas City Jail once, after a drunken brawl where the local tavern had been trashed. Grand was well known as a bit of a hot head and vigilante, taking matters into his own hands when it came to keeping UDAs, undocumented aliens, off his property. But the man had never been noted to use extreme measures and had not been cited for anything other than the brawl and tickets.

Jarrod stroked his fingers over his mustache as he brought up the next suspect…and then his blood boiled.

When Steve Wilds was nineteen, he had beat the crap out of a kid who'd apparently tried to force Catie to have sex in the back seat of his car at the drive-in. According to the police report, Steve had heard that Reggie Parker had been bragging he was going to "do her." Steve tracked them down and found Catie trying to fight the boy off. Steve punched the living daylights out of Parker, who'd ended up with stitches and a busted jaw. Because Steve had been nineteen, and Parker seventeen, Steve had been charged as an adult for assaulting a minor.

Jarrod gritted his teeth—he hoped to hell that Steve had done some damage to that SOB who'd tried to rape Catie. As far as Jarrod was concerned, he owed Steve for that one.

He read on, finding almost nothing of note that he didn't already know. Steve Wilds co-owned the Wilds Ranch with Catie, and had been operating in the red for the past few years. He'd spent some time in the hospital a few years back for a spinal cord injury, but with therapy he was back on his feet. Bank records showed normal fluctuations in the ranch and personal accounts until a sudden influx of cash—ten grand deposited last week.

Jarrod gave a low whistle. That was a good chunk of change for a rancher whose only known source of income was a spread running in the red.

When he clicked on information regarding the next suspect, Jarrod narrowed his eyes.

Jess Lawless had an absolutely clean record. Too clean. He was born and raised in Cheyenne, Wyoming, studied agribusiness at Auburn University, had an Arizona driver's license, and that was it—no other information was available on the ranch foreman, not even a traffic ticket. From Jarrod's conversations with Jake Reynolds, he agreed that something wasn't quite right about the cowboy. The man moved and looked like a regular cowhand, but there was just something else in the way he worked that told Jarrod there was more to Lawless than met the eye. But likely he'd have to dig deeper to find out.

Last was Ryan Forrester. When the deputy had been unavailable the first time an intruder was spotted on the MacLeod Ranch, an alarm had been triggered in the back of Jarrod's mind. He'd kept an eye on Forrester since then, and had become more suspicious and aware of the man's actions and mannerisms.

Jarrod shifted in his seat as he looked through the window of his office into the control room. He saw that it was still midday empty and returned his gaze to the computer.

Forrester's record was nicked and scarred, but nothing that would relieve him of duty. He'd been questioned for use of excessive force, but everything had been cleared. Bull Stevens, the previous Sheriff, had reprimanded Forrester for not being in his assigned location a couple of times. And Forrester had filed for Chapter thirteen bankruptcy protection the previous fall.

But what caught Jarrod's attention was the information that Brogan had dug up that wasn't in the deputy's work record.

Apparently, Forrester had the gambling bug.

* * * * *

"Oh, yes." Catie sighed with pleasure as she eased into the old-fashioned footed tub and luxuriated in the warm bathwater. "That's more like it."

After a long, tiring, Monday from hell, it was heaven to take a bubble bath. First she'd gotten into an argument with Steve because the big jerk refused to tell her where he'd gotten the money for the water heater; then one of the heifers had apparently eaten some locoweed and had to be put down; she'd ripped another good pair of jeans when she repaired the barbed wire fence that had been cut again; and on top of that, it looked like they were missing another ten head of cattle.

"Not going to think about any of that crap right now." Catie grabbed a luffa sponge from the soap tray and squirted her favorite vanilla musk gel on it. With energetic strokes, she scrubbed her skin until her body tingled.

It had been so long since they'd had hot water that she'd forgotten how wonderful it felt to relax in the tub after a hard day of ranch work. Even though he was keeping his trap shut on where he'd gotten the funds, she could almost forgive Steve for springing for the luxury of a new water heater. *Almost.*

Taking a deep breath of the vanilla-scented bubbles, she closed her eyes and leaned against the back of the old-fashioned footed tub, enjoying the silky feel of warm water against her skin. Water lapped at her nipples, causing them to harden into tight little nubs, reminding her of the way Jarrod had licked and sucked them to attention. She moved her hands to her breasts, cupping them, imaging that he was with her now, his muscular body pressed into hers, his cock as hard as cordwood against her belly.

But for once her own touch and mental fantasies failed to satisfy her. It was Jarrod that she wanted… She *needed* to have the man's hands on her body. She'd had the real thing, and now her imagination just wouldn't to. At least 'til she got the man out of her system.

"Dammit." With a frown she opened her eyes and scooted up in the tub. It really was starting to tick her off that she couldn't get him off her mind. What the hell was the matter with her? He was just a man, nothing special.

Yeah, right.

Instead of enjoying a nice, leisurely bath, Catie ended up rushing through the rest of it. She kept trying to shove

Jarrod out of her thoughts, but the bastard kept returning, not leaving her alone.

When she'd toweled off, she threw on her old cotton robe, yanked a comb through her wet hair and marched into her bedroom. She was pissed and horny, *not* a good combination. She'd put Jarrod off until Friday night and it was only Monday. How the hell was she going to make it until Friday without a good fuck?

But at the same time, she wondered how he'd managed to convince her to attend a dinner with the mayor. The *mayor* for crying out loud.

The piercing ring of the telephone was like a screech through Catie's mind. She checked the caller ID, but didn't recognize the number, and no name was shown. Catie snatched up the cordless, ready to take out her pent-up sexual frustration on the telemarketer who dared to interrupt her mental tirade. "Wilds."

"Yes. You are," Jarrod's deep voice rumbled over the phone.

"Jarrod." Warmth flushed over Catie, heating every cell, every pore on her body. "I'm what?" Dammit, but her brain always took a hike around him.

"Wild…in bed and out." His tone was throbbing with sensuality, and if she'd had panties on right then, they'd be soaked. God did he ever make her hot. "Sure you won't change your mind about dinner before Friday?"

It took all her resolve not to beg him to come over *now*. Instead, she somehow managed to keep her voice light and teasing. "It's a busy week, cowboy."

"What are you doing right now?"

A spark of mischief skittered through her belly. She grinned and perched on the edge of her bed. "I'm lying in my bed…absolutely naked."

Jarrod sucked in his breath, and it was a good heartbeat before he responded. "You'd better be careful, little wildcat. I'll be there faster than you can make yourself come."

Catie pulled at the tie of her robe, his words giving her an idea. "Have you ever had phone sex?"

"Uh, no."

"Ah." She slid off the robe and settled against the pillows on her bed. "So you're a phone sex virgin."

Jarrod gave a soft chuckle. "Been a long time since I was called that."

"Well it's time you lose that cherry." Catie cupped one of her breasts with her free hand. "I'll tell you what I'm doing. I'm playing with my nipples, imagining that you're sucking them."

"Damn, woman." Jarrod groaned, and she could visualize the raging desire in his expression. "I can picture your pussy. So pink and wet, just for me."

"Oh, yeah." Moisture flooded her core and cool air brushed her pussy as she spread her legs. "Where are you right now?"

"In my study," he said like he was gritting his teeth, "with a hard-on the size of Texas."

Catie laughed. "Well, then. We need to do something about that."

"You coming over here, or am I going there?"

"Neither." She rubbed her hand up and down her flat belly. "Take off your clothes, cowboy."

A pause, and then he said, "Honey, I don't know what you do to me, but I can't believe I'm actually considering it."

"Just take off your clothes, big guy."

"Hold on." Jarrod grunted and she heard the rustle of fabric, the faint thump of boots on tile.

While she waited, Catie closed her eyes and tweaked first one nipple, then the next as she pictured his hard muscled body, naked and waiting for her. A part of her wanted to give in and meet with him before Friday. But she couldn't take the chance of starting to like the man *too* much, or give him the wrong idea—that they were anything more than friends and occasional lovers.

"Ready." Jarrod's voice interrupted her train of thought. "I just need your pussy here so that I can fuck you senseless."

"Mmmmm." She squirmed on the bed, dying for the feel of him inside her. "Grab your cock and imagine that my tongue is licking over it like you're a super-sized ice cream cone."

"And woman, do you ever have a talented tongue." he murmured. "My turn. I want you to finger your pussy." Jarrod paused and she dipped her fingers into her slick folds. He lowered his voice and added, "Now taste yourself for me."

A small gasp escaped Catie's throat at what he suggested and she hesitated. She'd smelled her own musk on her hand, and tasted herself on Jarrod's tongue, but lick her own fingers?

"Come on, honey." His groan was low and primal.

"All right, just for you." She smiled and brought her forefinger to her mouth and sucked on it with a smack loud enough for him to hear over the phone. "Mmmm. It's like tasting myself on your cock."

"Damn but you make me hot." Jarrod's breathing was growing harsh. "I want to fuck you. I want to fuck you more than anything."

A thrill coursed through her, a heady feeling of power. The knowledge that she could turn this man on as much as he turned her on was addicting, like the most potent of drugs.

"Are you stroking your cock?" Her fingers found her clit and resumed the familiar motion that made her feel so good. "I'm fingering myself, Jarrod."

"Yeah. I want to come inside you, Catie."

"That's good. So good." She clenched the phone tighter as her arousal grew. Her own breathing became more labored as her finger dipped into her core and she spread her juices over her clit. "I'm picturing you and that big cock of yours. You're sliding it into my pussy and you're fucking me hard and fast."

"What if I put my finger up your ass while I fuck you," Jarrod murmured. "Would you like that?"

A wild moaned slipped through her lips at the thought of having him in her ass and her pussy at once. Her fingers stroked her clit harder and faster, bringing her closer to the peak.

"Would you, Catie?" His tone was gruff. "Or how about if I rammed my cock in your ass, would you like that?"

"Yes, dammit." She had to force the words out as she began to climax. "I'd like you to fuck me every way possible." The orgasm took hold of her body, her muscles clenching from head to toe. "Jarrod!" she shouted as she came. Her fingers continued, drawing out her orgasm, while her body shuddered and trembled.

Through the rush of blood in her ears she heard Jarrod's groan of release, his heavy breathing, and then his husky laugh.

"You're amazing." He sounded sated, but like he could go another round or two. "No other woman on the face of god's green earth could make me jack off while on the telephone."

Laughter and pleasure filled Catie. "Thanks for the great phone sex, cowboy," she murmured. And then she hung up on him.

Chapter Eight

Catie put on a pair of small gold hoop earrings, spritzed on her vanilla musk cologne, and then checked her appearance in the mirror. She rarely wore makeup, but wondered if today she should make an exception considering how she looked—like she was nervous or something. Her cheeks were so pale it made her freckles stand out across her nose.

What the hell, she might as well go for it. She settled for dusting a bronze blush on her cheekbones, a light coat of brown mascara, and lipstick in a burnt cinnamon shade. And why not—a little sable liner along her lashes, just like the Avon lady had shown her.

Frowning at her reflection, Catie smoothed the skirt of the strapless black dress that came to mid-thigh. It wasn't an expensive dress, but it had a classic look that supposedly made it appropriate for any occasion. Truth be told, she didn't give a damn about that—she just hoped that it would make Jarrod so out of his mind with lust that he'd want to fuck her as soon as he saw her.

It had been a week since she'd seen Jarrod, and she was regretting agreeing to go with him to the mayor's dinner. She wanted him so badly she didn't think she could wait until the dinner was over.

Her frown turned into a grin as she thought about how much fun it would be to find a secluded corner in the mayor's house, and fuck Jarrod there. With all their dirty talk on the phone every night this week, she was so hot for him she'd probably jump him the moment he arrived. She almost wished that tomorrow she didn't have to go to Dee and Jake's reception. Jarrod had agreed to go with her, but right now she wanted him all to herself so that she could enjoy his body — and especially his cock.

Catie grabbed her black beaded handbag, tossed in the lipstick, and walked through the quiet house, wondering where it was that Steve had been going off to every night. He must have started working some kind of side job that he wasn't telling her about. How else could he have afforded the water heater? And why would he be so secretive about what he was doing?

When she reached the window that looked out onto the front yard, she pushed the curtain aside and peered through the clouded pane and into the night. A pair of headlights cut through the darkness, headed up the dirt road to her ranch house. Her hand automatically went to her ear and she pulled at the gold earring.

Jarrod. Catie held her purse tight to her belly with one hand, as if it could calm the sudden flutter there, and stepped back from the window. She took a deep breath and closed her eyes.

He's just a man. Nothing special.

The roar of a truck's engine came closer. She remained still, almost unable to move while she listened to the sound of gravel crunching under big tires...the engine cutting off...the slam of a door...and then the sound of heavy boots on her porch steps.

What's the matter with me?

The screen door creaked and then a loud knock sounded. Catie's eyes flew open and she stared at the door. Why did it feel like everything would change if she walked through that door and into Jarrod's arms tonight?

Stop being so damn stupid!

Another knock jolted Catie into action, and she moved forward and reached for the worn brass knob. When she opened the door, she almost forgot to breathe.

Jarrod was dressed in a black suit, his mouth curved into a sensual smile and his green eyes positively smoldering. He looked like he could have stepped out of the pages of some high-fashioned men's magazine.

"You're so gorgeous, honey." He reached for her, slid his fingers into her hair, and cupped the back of her head. "Damn but I've missed you."

"Hey, sexy," was all she had a chance to say before he brought his mouth to hers. He moved his lips over hers in a soft and sensuous kiss that stole every bit of her remaining breath. A moan rose up within Catie, and she barely realized she had wrapped her arms around his neck and pulled him tighter to her.

His kiss deepened, her thoughts spinning as she parted her lips and he slipped his tongue into her mouth. She welcomed him, drawing him deeper into her. Today he tasted of cinnamon and his own elemental flavor. Jarrod's arousal was clear, his cock big and hard against her belly. Her core flooded at the thought of having that awesome length deep inside her again. It'd been too long since she'd had him.

Faintly she heard something clatter to the floor, but the whole world could come crashing down for all she cared. The only thing that mattered was the feel of his man in her arms, how good he tasted, his masculine scent, and the way he held her against him.

When he broke the kiss, he pressed his forehead to hers. Catie opened her eyes to see his sexy smile so close to her lips. Feeling dazed and breathless, she swallowed, trying to calm the emotions rushing through her.

Not emotions—*lust*. That was all she felt for him…lust.

He trailed his knuckles along her jaw line. "You ready to head on out, little wildcat?"

"Yeah." Her voice was barely a husky whisper.

Snap out of it! she shouted in her head.

Fixing a flirty smile on her face, Catie pushed herself away from Jarrod. "I'm ready if you are."

"You don't know how ready I am." He winked, but then knelt and started picking up items from the floor—and Catie realized what the clatter had been. She'd dropped her purse, scattering her ID, lipstick, and change all over the floor. Before she had a chance to help him, he had everything gathered up. "You carry a pocketknife?" he asked as he dropped it into her purse and stood.

"I'm pretty handy with it." She shrugged and took her purse from him. "And it was a gift from someone who was like a mom to me. She lived down at the Old Karchner Ranch, but she died a while back. Some other woman lives there now. Hispanic, I think. I haven't gotten to know her. It's—well, just too hard to go down there, you know? I always think of Mrs. Karchner."

"Ah." Jarrod glanced around the small living room. "Where's your brother?"

"Hell if I know." Catie brushed a strand of hair behind her ear. "He's been gone every night and won't tell me where. I think he's got a side job and just doesn't want to tell me about it for some macho reason."

Something flickered in Jarrod's eyes, but then it was gone. "Let's go before I decide to forget all about the damn dinner." He brushed his lips over hers. "'Cause the way you look tonight, honey, we'll be lucky if we even make it to the mayor's house."

"Who needs him anyway?" She flicked her tongue against the corner of his mouth, her naked pussy aching beneath her dress.

He groaned and caught her face in his palms. "I brought a little something for you."

With a naughty grin Catie placed her hand against his cock and felt its rigid length beneath his slacks. "You sure did, but I'd say that's more than a *little* something."

Jarrod captured her hand in one of his and held it to his chest, while his other hand dug into his suit jacket and pulled out a long jeweler's box.

Catie's eyes widened and she tried to step back, but he held her hand too tightly against him. "I can't accept a gift from you, Jarrod." She swallowed as she looked up at him.

"Just open it." He placed the box to her free hand until she took it, and then released her other hand.

Curiosity won out, and she opened the box. Lying upon a bed of black velvet was a necklace, each link a tiny heart, and each heart with a diamond chip at its center. "It's gorgeous." She snapped the box shut and handed it back to him. "It's too expensive. You can't give me this and I can't accept it."

"Let's just see how it looks." He reopened the box and unhooked each end of the necklace from within its velvet nest.

"No." Catie shook her head. "I've known you for less than two weeks. And I already told you, no commitment. Of any kind."

"I'm not asking for commitment." His smile was so erotic her nipples became diamond points against the thin fabric of her dress. "Just wear the damn necklace. Humor me, all right?"

"Okay." Raising her chin, she gave him a mischievous smile. "Under one condition."

Jarrod quirked his brow. "What's that?"

"You have to promise to let me give you head."

His mouth curved up into a grin. "No problem."

"While we're at the mayor's house."

"Uh, no."

"Either that, or you have to fuck me." A devious feeling rose up within her. "Somewhere very public."

* * * * *

Jarrod and Catie arrived at the mayor's house promptly at seven. He glanced over at her in the passenger seat just as she bit her lower lip, and he realized that his feisty wildcat was nervous.

Well, good. Maybe she'd get that crazy public sex idea out of her beautiful little head. He couldn't believe he'd agreed to Catie's condition—the woman was making him certifiably nuts. If he didn't watch it, his dick was going to get him into serious trouble.

Hell, he was already courting disaster by dating a suspect's sister. And after the new evidence that Deputy Forrester had turned up that morning, it was looking more and more like Steve Wilds was in some seriously deep shit.

He reached over and squeezed Catie's hand. "Ready?"

A car passed, the headlights illuminating her delicate features as her eyes met his. She raised her chin, a proud tilt to her head. "What if I don't fit in here? I'm just a rancher —"

Jarrod caught her face in his hands and silenced her with a long, hard kiss. When he pulled away, he looked into her eyes that glittered in the near darkness. "Honey, you're smart and sexy...you fit me perfectly."

"But —"

He pressed his thumb against her lips, silencing her protest. "Just be the beautiful and confident Catie Wilds that I can't get enough of."

Jarrod helped her out of his truck, and she held his hand tight as they walked up to the home of Douglas Mayor Eduardo Montaño, one of the biggest houses in the area. A well-known businessman even before becoming mayor, Montaño owned a popular Mexican restaurant in town.

Catie's chin rose higher as a young man greeted them at the door, and then escorted into a formal living room already filled with guests. Jarrod squeezed her hand and felt her relax, as though his confidence was transferred to her. The mayor's home was decorated much as his restaurant was, in bold colors, portraits of bullfighters and other décor that spoke of his Hispanic heritage.

"Savage." Montaño approached them, holding out one hand. "It is good to see you again."

"Montaño." Jarrod grasped the mayor's hand in a firm grip, then released it to introduce Catie. "Have you met Catie Wilds? She and her brother own a ranch outside town."

Montaño clasped Catie's hand and smiled. "A pleasure, señorita."

Her smile was radiant as she responded in kind to the mayor. Before Jarrod had the chance to say another word, Montaño took it upon himself to introduce Catie to each of the other guests, which included council members and a couple of local business owners and their spouses. All Jarrod could do was follow like some third wheel, but every now and then Catie would toss him a look that said *don't forget your promise to fuck me in public*, and it was all he could do to keep from sporting a hard-on the entire evening.

Throughout the night, the way that the other men looked at Catie, Jarrod couldn't decide whether he should want to kick their asses or stick out his chest with pride. She was a knockout in her tiny black dress and high heels, clearly the most beautiful woman there. Her hair shimmered like gold floss in the light of the chandeliers, and her brown eyes seemed bigger and more luminous than ever. The delicate chain of golden hearts and diamonds glittered with every move she made.

Truth be told, he had wondered what Catie might come up with tonight as frank as she was in conversation. That was one of the things that he loved about her, the way that she spoke her mind without worrying about what others might think.

When they were seated for dinner, Jarrod and Catie found themselves in the middle of one side of the table set for twelve.

"I've never been to such a fancy dinner," Catie whispered to Jarrod as they were served cold gazpacho in footed silver bowls. "I'm afraid I'm going to do something stupid."

"You'll do fine, honey." He settled his hand on her knee beneath the tablecloth, enjoying her slight gasp as he moved his fingers to the warm flesh inside her thigh. "Just do what I do."

"All right." She smiled and moved her hand to his lap, right on his cock. "Like that?"

Jarrod's cock jerked and hardened at her touch, and he fought the urge to see if the people seated to either side of them could see what she was doing to him. He lowered his lids, his gaze burning into hers. "Eat your dinner."

She spoke so softly that he almost had to read her lips, as she said, "I'd rather eat you."

He damn near groaned out loud at the thought of those lips and that soft mouth going down on him. The councilman on Catie's other side took that moment to ask her a question, and her teasing brown eyes were drawn from Jarrod.

As they ate dinner, conversation ranged from politics to various other problems that plagued the border community. Catie made it a point to torture Jarrod with a hand on his lap, or sliding off her shoe and running her silken foot along his ankle. At one point she even leaned in, her vanilla musk scent sweeping over him as she whispered, "I want to fuck you now."

Jarrod just about choked on his mouthful of grilled salmon. He retaliated by sliding his fingers along the inside of her thigh, planning to rub his fingers along the crotch of her panties—only to have his fingers come in contact with her bare pussy. His cock hardened to the point he'd thought for sure it would thrust right through the material of his dress slacks.

When the topic of cattle rustling came up, Jarrod tried to head it off with, "We're working on it," but each person at the table seemed to have some comment.

"Well something needs to be done, and soon," Catie added to the conversation and Jarrod tensed beside her.

Eduardo Montaño's eyes rested on her. "What would you suggest?"

She set her fork on the edge of her plate, her gaze steady as it met the mayor's. "It's obvious that it can't be completely an outside job." Conversation around the table quieted as Catie continued, "I believe it's someone familiar with folks in the area, someone who knows how and when to strike."

Montaño nodded. "Do you think it could be anyone you know?"

Jarrod was practically holding his breath as he watched Catie brush a strand of hair behind her ear, a troubled look crossing her face. "I can't imagine it would be any of the ranchers in our area. They're all good people, and they've all been hit. But whoever it is, the law should lock them up for good once the bastard's caught."

Murmurs of agreement came from around the table, and Jarrod took the opportunity to ask what everyone thought about the Cardinals' chances of making the playoffs that year.

"Cardinals?" Catie scoffed, her brown eyes meeting his. "Have you had a look at the way their defense has been playing lately?"

"The 49ers are going to put the Cardinals away in the next game," Montaño agreed.

While the banter continued Jarrod studied Catie, who passionately participated in the debate. He hadn't even realized that she was a football fan. How much more of a perfect woman could he have asked for?

He just hoped to god that Catie wasn't going to hate him if he ended up having to arrest her brother.

When a decadent chocolate mousse was served for dessert, Catie found her opportunity. Or rather, she made it.

"Ow," she said, just loud enough to be heard over the appreciative murmurs around the table. "Something's in my eye."

"Can I do something for you?" Montaño asked as Catie held her hand over her eye.

"Just point me to the bathroom, and I'll take care of it." She started to push back her chair, but Jarrod was already standing and pulling it out for her.

"Do you mind helping me?" she asked him, keeping the one eye squeezed shut.

"Of course." His expression was concerned, yet the flare in his green eyes told her he knew she was up to something. Jarrod pressed his hand to the small of her back as he guided her across the massive house and into the opulent rose-scented bathroom.

The moment they were inside, she locked the door and wrapped her arms around his neck and grinned. "We had a bargain, lawman."

He groaned, but his big hands gripped her hips, the heat burning through her thin dress like a pair of branding irons. "You're such a little shit."

"Enough talk." Her hands moved to his belt, and a small thrill charged through her at the feel of his already huge cock beneath his dress slacks. She was so wet and turned-on she couldn't wait to get him inside her. "Just fuck me, big guy."

Jarrod yanked up her dress and rubbed her bare ass with his palms as she freed his length and pushed his slacks down around his hips. A sigh of sheer lust escaped her as she slid her fingers up and down his rigid cock.

He grasped her ass and raised her up onto the marble countertop, and she jerked her attention to his face. His eyes burned a deep, passionate jade as he pushed her thighs apart and pressed himself against her pussy.

"Damn, you drive me crazy, woman." He brushed the head of his cock against the swollen lips of her pussy. He stroked her clit with the purple head of his rod, and then eased it down to her dripping wet core. "What I'd do for you."

"Then fuck me already." Catie moaned and braced her hands on the countertop, the marble cold and erotic beneath her bare ass.

In one smooth motion, Jarrod drilled his cock into her pussy. She gasped at the incredible sensation of having him fill her again. Damn but she'd missed him inside her this week.

"Oh, God, that feels good. So, so good." She watched his cock moving in and out of her pussy. "More. I need *more*."

He grasped his hands beneath her knees, drawing her up and widening her to take more of him. Harder and harder he thrust inside her, his balls slapping her ass, their breathing coming in harsh gasps.

"Yes, that's it." She wished she could get her hands on his hard muscled body. Wished she could rake her nails down his back as he fucked her.

"I'm going to come, honey." His voice was low and hoarse. "Come with me."

"I'm ready." Catie's breathing was labored as she felt her muscles begin to clench. "Now, Jarrod. *Now.*"

Just as she felt a scream rise in her throat, Jarrod placed his mouth over hers. His kiss was strong and fierce, swallowing her cries and feeding her his own as their bodies jerked and throbbed against one another. For a moment they remained in that intimate embrace, the smell of his come mingling with the scent of her own juices.

Jarrod's eyes locked with hers, their chests rising and falling with equally labored breaths. And then he smiled, the look in his eyes purely male sexual satisfaction. Catie couldn't help but return his smile.

"Damn that was fun," she said, and had the intense desire to giggle.

He grinned and pressed a kiss to her forehead. "Talk about an understatement."

When they both had caught their breath, they cleaned up. Catie rubbed her eye to make it look red, like she'd really had something in her eye.

Jarrod shook his head as he checked his own appearance in the mirror and then looked down like he was making sure there was no wet spot on his fly. "I can't believe I just fucked you in the mayor's house."

"A deal's a deal," she murmured as she reached up and kissed him.

Chapter Nine

Catie woke the following morning with Jarrod's arms wrapped tight around her, one hand cupping her breast. He had a leg hooked over hers, and his erect cock pressed tight to her backside. His face was buried in the crook of her neck, his warm breath brushing over her skin. It felt so good waking up with him...

Wait. What the hell was she doing? Twice now she'd broken her no-spending-the-night rule. Twice with the same man, no less.

When he'd asked her to spend the night after they'd left the mayor's house, she caved plain as could be. Maybe she should have seen him during the week, 'cause she would have gotten him a little more out of her system. As it was, she couldn't seem to satisfy her craving for his taste, his smell, or the feel of him deep inside her.

Yeah, that was it. The sex. When she'd had enough of him she'd break it off like she always did.

A contented sigh eased through her as she allowed herself to relax in his arms. Her muscles felt the good ache of a long night of fucking, and the smell of their sex surrounded her, filling her senses.

Jarrod stirred, his cock rubbing up against her ass, and her pussy grew wet with the desire to have him yet again. Her nipples beaded, and need curled through her belly. Damn, but she had to get through this quick before she fell in lo—

No. Not going there. Ever. I'm not an idiot like either of my parents were.

His lips and tongue began a moist trail down the curve of her neck. "Good morning, beautiful."

"Hi, Sheriff." Catie shivered and closed her eyes, trying to fight off the deeper feelings of intimacy surging through her. Feelings that she didn't believe in, that she couldn't allow herself to acknowledge.

"I think I like waking up with you in my arms," Jarrod's husky voice murmured, and she had to bite her tongue not to agree. He squeezed and flexed the sweetly tender flesh of her breast, and her nipple sprang to life beneath his touch.

"Well, don't get used to it," Catie replied instead, but her voice wavered as her arousal grew.

"Don't count on that, honey." He rubbed the inside of his thigh along her hip while rubbing his erection along her backside. A moan escaped and she arched into the hand fondling her breast while her ass pressed even harder against his cock.

Before she had a chance to catch her breath, Jarrod rolled her over and slid between her thighs. He propped his arms to either side of her, his brown hair tousled and his morning beard making him appear dark and dangerous. He just looked down at her with sleepy morning arousal in his green eyes, and that sexy smile that took her breath away.

And something more that she definitely did not want to see.

Catie squirmed, wrapping her legs around his hips, and tried to reach for his cock. "Just fuck me already."

"Uh-uh." In a quick movement he grabbed both her wrists and pinned them over her head. "Let's take this slow and easy."

His mouth captured her protest and turned it into a moan that burned through her soul. His kiss was gentle but demanding, encouraging and insistent all at once.

Catie couldn't think any longer, she could only feel...his lips, soft yet firm against hers, the rough scrape of his stubble against her cheeks and her mouth, the taste and smell of him that flooded her senses.

She whimpered, clamping her legs tighter around his hips, pressing his erection to her belly. But he ignored her body's pleas, torturing her with the kiss, filling her mouth with his tongue and his taste.

When he finally raised his head, she couldn't seem to catch her breath. He studied her with heavy-lidded eyes, one hand still pinning both her wrists above her head, the other stroking her hair from her face.

"You are so beautiful, honey." His voice was a sensual purr that shimmered through her body in waves, a sensation she'd never felt before.

"Please." She swallowed, not knowing what she was begging him for. To make love to her? To stop making her feel like she could fall in...

No. She just wanted him to fuck her good and hard.

Jarrod smiled as though he'd heard the thoughts she wouldn't allow herself to finish. "You're mine, Catie Wilds." His expression turned positively possessive, even predatory. "Don't think for one moment you aren't."

She shook her head, but he only smiled again and stilled her with another soul-searing, spine-tingling, world-ending kiss. Everything melted around her and she was only aware of his lips and tongue against her skin as he moved his mouth to her ear, dipping inside and then nipping her lope with his teeth.

"Jarrod." Catie could hardly catch her breath, and forget about being able to form a single thought. "Please."

"Tell me what you want." His mouth, tongue and teeth continued down her neck to her shoulder. "What do you need?"

"You—I need your cock inside me." She arched her back and cried out as he captured her nipple between his teeth and gently bit. "Fuck me."

"That's not what you need." His tongue laved her nipple, first hard, then gentle. "Tell me what you really need."

"What—what the hell are you talking about?" Damn but she couldn't even think, she had to have him so badly.

He moved to her other nipple, giving it the same attention he'd showered on the first. Laving it, sucking it, nipping at it. "This isn't just about sex anymore, honey."

She barely realized he had released her hands as he moved his mouth down her flat belly, over her shaved mound and to her leg. "Yes." Catie gasped as Jarrod's tongue flicked along the inside of her thigh. "I mean yes, it is just about fucking."

"Uh-uh." He continued swirling his tongue close to the puffy lips of her pussy, but not licking her clit like she wanted him to. "You can deny it all you want, but this is a hell of a lot more."

"Damn you, Jarrod Savage." Emotion and sensation whirled through Catie as he tortured her with his words and tongue. "I told you I've never believed in commitment, or anything that goes along with it."

He raised himself up on his elbows and his mouth quirked into a grin, his expression confident and cocksure. "But that was before you met me." He trailed a finger down her shaved pussy and touched her clit, and she nearly came off the bed with the intense sensations shooting through her.

Before she could tell him what a cocky bastard he was, he lowered his head and lapped at her pussy and she cried out from the excruciating pleasure. Oh, God did his tongue ever feel good on her clit as he licked and sucked, bringing her close to orgasm, and then backing off and starting the whole thing over again. She slid her hands in his thick hair, welcoming the distraction from their conversation, not wanting to examine the feelings growing inside her.

"Jarrod, please." Her hands clenched tighter in his hair, her thighs trembling from the orgasm that was almost about to overtake her. "Please make me come."

A growl rumbled from his chest as he slid both palms under her ass and buried his face hard against her pussy.

Catie screamed, her body jerking hard with every aftershock of her release. It seemed like her climax would never end. Her eyesight blurred, and she couldn't see or hear, only feel. He continued on, sucking and licking her clit until a second orgasm sent her reeling beyond the first.

For a moment she could only stay there, perched on a precipice of sensations, unable to move. Gradually she came back down, her breathing harsh, heart pounding and blood rushing in her ears. Her vision cleared and her awareness of the world around her returned just as Jarrod eased up her body and propped himself above her. He watched her, an almost serious expression on his handsome face.

Lowering his weight so that he was pressed against her, he reached up and stroked her hair out of her face. "My little wildcat."

"No." She shook her head, not wanting him to voice the emotion she saw in his eyes. "Don't go there."

Jarrod smiled. "Whether you want to hear it or not, I'm going to tell you exactly where we're headed." He trailed his thumb along her lips, a slow and sensuous movement that caused her to catch her breath. "I'm in love with you, Catie Wilds."

"You haven't known me long enough to say that." Her lower lip trembled. "It's just the sex. We're good in bed."

"Listen to me." Jarrod put his hand over her mouth, his calloused fingers warm against her lips. "I knew from the moment you walked into my office. You're my woman."

Catie widened her eyes and tried to speak, but he only pressed his hand tighter to her mouth.

"I know you need time, and I'll give it to you." His smile was gentle, yet determined. "But you're not going to keep pushing me away, and you're not going to keep pretending this is all about sex." She tried to shake her head, but he moved his hands and caught her face between his palms. "You'd better get used to it, honey, 'cause you're my woman, and I'm your man."

His kiss was hard and possessive, melting away her automatic denial. She gave into the sensations, and somewhere deep in her heart, she reveled in the knowledge that this man had declared his love to her. That out of any woman he could have chosen, he loved *her*.

God. She was losing her mind. And the next thing she knew, she'd be losing her heart, too.

"This isn't fucking, Catie." He positioned his cock at the entrance to her core, his eyes locked with hers. "I'm making love to you."

Jarrod plunged his cock inside her pussy and she automatically raised her hips to meet him. He was such a perfect fit. And somehow it felt more intense, more pleasurable than it ever had before. As if knowing he loved her made their sex even better.

Making love.

Unable to take her eyes from his as he thrust with slow and deep strokes, Catie bit her lip to hold back any words that might decide to spill out on their own. He smiled and brought his mouth to hers, licking her lip where she was biting it. She wrapped her arms around his neck, holding on tight as she opened up to his tongue, and maybe even to the sweet emotions sweeping through her heart and soul.

This time her orgasm came out of nowhere. Fireworks exploded in her mind, brilliant colors and flashes of light that rocked her straight to her core. The walls of her channel contracted, gripping his cock with every pulse of her release.

"I love you, Catie," Jarrod murmured, his words uneven with his harsh breathing. And then he groaned with his orgasm, his cock throbbing inside her as he came.

He rolled over onto his side, pulling her with him, but keeping his cock within her pussy. He held her tight to his chest, their sweaty flesh pressed close, enveloping her in his strong arms. "You're mine, little wildcat. All mine."

* * * * *

While Catie sat beside him on the drive to the Flying M Ranch, Jarrod wondered what was going on in her gorgeous head. He had a good idea that she was sorting out her feelings for him, yet trying to keep from acknowledging them. But as far as he was concerned, it was only a matter of time.

Of course if he ended up having to arrest her brother, that might put a bit of a damper on their relationship.

She'd been fairly subdued as he drove her to the Wilds Ranch to change and get ready for the MacLeod-Reynolds shindig. Steve Wilds had been there, but the man hadn't had much to say, and seemed to have a lot on his mind. Jarrod liked Steve, and his gut told him that Wilds was a good man. But from experience Jarrod knew too well how a good man could end up in a bad situation and not know how to dig himself out.

Outside the November day was cloudy, but it didn't look like it would rain, at least until late evening. Acres of dry grass rolled by on the two mile drive, populated by herds of cattle. Jarrod gritted his teeth at the thought of what he might have to do soon. A little more evidence and he wouldn't have a choice.

Catie seemed to tense the closer they got to MacLeod Ranch, and one hand moved to her neck to play with the heart necklace he'd convinced her to wear. She clenched her other hand so tight on her lap that her knuckles whitened against her denim skirt. Her blonde hair shone in the sunlight and her chocolate eyes looked so big she appeared younger than she was. She had flawless skin, a natural beauty that didn't need makeup, and the freckles across her nose were just damn irresistible.

Jarrod took one hand off the steering wheel and placed it over hers. "You all right, honey?"

"Why wouldn't I be?" She gave a forced smile. "It's just a party."

He turned his attention back to the dirt road as he made the turn into the Flying M Ranch. "It bothers you that your friend has gotten married."

"I'm happy for Dee."

"But you're worried about her for the same reason you're worried about us." He glanced at Catie as she raised her chin, a defiant look on her face.

"You know my history, Jarrod," she said as he looked back to the road.

"It's not *your* history. Can't you get that through your thick little head?" He gave her a crooked grin. "It's a beautiful head, but damn thick."

Catie's lips twitched. "You'd better watch it, or I'll come up with something really good to do to you while we're at the barbeque."

"Uh-oh." Jarrod shook his head as he guided the truck up to the MacLeod house. "You've got that look in your eyes again. Don't tell me you're gonna try to corner me in the bathroom again."

She reached over and rubbed his already lengthening cock through his jeans. "Oh, just you wait. I'll think of something even better."

Jarrod groaned as he pulled the truck alongside a row of vehicles parked in the massive front yard. Obviously it was going to be one hell of a party — there had to be fifty vehicles there. Off to the right, to the side of the barn and extensive corrals, huge awnings had been pitched and folks milled around, chatting and carrying plates heaped with food.

"Looks like everyone and their mother is here," Catie said as he opened the door and climbed out.

He took her hand as she followed him out the driver side door, enjoying the feel of her small fingers within his. Her skirt hiked up and his cock jerked at the thought of what was under that skirt—nothing but bare pussy.

"Later, Sheriff." With a naughty smile, Catie pulled her skirt lower, hiding that delicious prize. "If you're a good boy, I might just let you sample some."

Jarrod groaned and swatted her on the ass while he slammed the door shut. "If you're not a good girl, I'm gonna have to turn you over my knee and spank you."

She grinned up at him as he draped his arm around her shoulders. "You keep promising and not delivering."

Even though he was determined that she take their relationship seriously, he was glad to see her feisty personality and sass had returned. He held her close as they walked toward the crowd, the sound of voices and laughter filling the chilly November air. Children played Frisbee and football out in the field, and to the side of the tents a few folks apparently had a hot game of horseshoes going on. A faint breeze carried with it smells of grilled beef and roasted chicken, along with the tangy scent of barbeque and spice.

Catie was her animated self as she greeted people she knew and was introduced to those she didn't. Jarrod could hardly tear his gaze from her beautiful smile long enough to do his own share of socializing. It felt good to be with her anywhere they went.

But damn, he couldn't wait to get her alone again.

Chapter Ten

Catie made polite talk as she worked her way through the crowd with Jarrod at her side. They stopped to talk with Kev Grand for a moment. Catie was almost surprised to see him, since he'd been after Dee himself for so long, but the man was his usual down-home-boy self.

Everyone seemed to want to make small talk with Catie and Jarrod, but she was dying to find her best friend — to see if she was really happy being married. When Deputy Ryan Forrester greeted them, it was all Catie could do to patiently wait at Jarrod's side while they bullshitted about one thing or another.

Finally, Catie spotted Dee MacLeod-Reynolds in the crowd and her heart rate picked up. She asked Ryan to excuse them as she grabbed Jarrod's hand and then led him toward where her friend stood with her new husband. They were across the way, standing near where a dance would be later that evening. A makeshift dance floor had been laid out beneath a massive tent, with speakers and other soundstage equipment for a live band.

Jarrod's hand tightened around Catie's as they walked toward the newlyweds. Dee seemed more beautiful than ever, her hair tumbling down her back in a fall of auburn, a radiant smile on her face. Jake was watching Dee with pride in his eyes, and a look that said *this is my woman*.

Dee's husband was certainly a handsome man, *although not nearly as gorgeous as my man*.

The thought made Catie falter and only Jarrod's grip on her hand kept her moving forward until they reached her friend.

When she turned and saw Catie, delight filled Dee's expression. "Where the heck have you been, Sweetpea?"

"So you went and did it, girlfriend." Catie hugged Dee tight, inhaling her friend's familiar orange blossom scent. "Are you keeping that man in line?"

Dee laughed as she pulled away. "It's an uphill battle," she replied with a grin at Jake.

"Well, be sure and call me if you need any help." Catie turned from Dee to face Jake, and poked her finger at his chest. "Now listen good, cowboy. You treat my best friend right, or I'm gonna kick your ass."

Amusement sparked in his gray eyes as he gave her a solemn nod. "Of course, Sweetpea."

"Only Dee is allowed to call me that." Catie planted her hands on her hips and gave him a pretend glare. "And if you don't behave, I'll tell everyone what her pet name is for you."

Jake cast Dee a look over Catie's head. "You didn't."

Dee reached up and planted a kiss on his cheek. "Sorry, baby. I did." He rolled his eyes and Dee laughed.

"Congratulations, Reynolds." Jarrod stepped forward and offered his hand to Jake. "Snagged yourself one beautiful woman."

"That I did." Jake grinned and clasped Jarrod's hand and then released it. "I hear you caught one of your own," he added with a wink at Catie.

Jarrod hooked his arm around her shoulders and pulled her close. "Got that right."

"Well, he'd like to think so." Heat flushed Catie's cheeks and she elbowed him in the side. "Trust living in a small community to spread crazy rumors."

"Now what was Lawless telling me?" Jarrod said to Jake. "Tossed your woman over your shoulder and carted her off to Vegas to get married?"

"Yup." Jake caught a handful of Dee's auburn hair and tugged on it. "Wasn't about to let her get away."

Jarrod looked down at Catie with a teasing grin on his face. "So that's how it's done."

She gave a loud sniff and folded her arms across her chest. "Try it and you won't be walking straight, Sheriff Savage."

Jake chuckled and laughter glimmered in Dee's light green eyes.

"When's Trace coming home?" Catie asked, anxious to change the subject. "Your sister's been in Europe for what, four years?"

"Yeah, she's been all over the place, working in public relations for a software company." A slight cloud passed over Dee's expression. "Right now she's in England and will be home sometime before Christmas. I really wish she could have been here today."

Catie reached out and squeezed her friend's arm. "She'll be here soon, and you can catch up then."

"Way to go Reynolds," a deep masculine voice interrupted, and Catie's eyes cut to Jess Lawless as he extended his hand to Jake. He gave Dee that sexy grin that used to make Catie's panties wet. "'Bout time someone roped in that gal."

Dee shook her finger at him, her lips curved into a smile. "This gal is your boss."

As Jess congratulated the newlyweds, Catie's gaze went from Jess to Jake, and then rested on Jarrod. Good Lord — talk about a trio of handsome male specimens. All were around the six foot range, all big and muscular, and all drop-dead gorgeous cowboys.

Yet the only man who gave her any kind of thrill now was Jarrod. It was like he filled her senses, fit her life in ways she never dreamed a man could.

Somehow the thought both frightened and comforted her, a strange and unsettling feeling that she couldn't decide what to do with. The weight of his arm around her shoulders felt *right*, and she found herself wanting to lean into him. Wanting to draw strength from him and let him lead. Wanting to not always have to be the willful woman she prided herself on being.

If she allowed herself to give into these feelings, would she be giving up her own identity?

Catie pushed the thoughts to the back of her mind. She couldn't deal with them now. They were too new, too fresh, too…alien.

Her gaze roamed the crowd and she spotted her brother talking to a curvy woman with black hair and a beautiful smile. The way the woman was looking at Steve, and the slightly goofy expression on his face, made Catie snap to attention.

"I'll be right back," she said to Jarrod. Before he could respond, she slipped out from under his arm and made a beeline for Steve.

He was making such goo-goo eyes at the gal that he didn't even notice Catie's approach, so she butted right in. "Hi." She grinned as she stuck out her hand, offering it to the brunette. "I'm Catie. Steve's sister."

The woman grasped Catie's hand, her smile warm and friendly. "Natalie Garcia. I just bought the old Karchner place a couple miles north of your ranch." Natalie released Catie's hand and turned her dark eyes on Steve, who had a sheepish look on his face. "Your brother has mentioned you quite often."

Before Catie could respond, *funny, but I've never heard of you*, Natalie hooked one finger on the back of a wheelchair beside her, drawing Catie's eyes to a boy of about nine or ten years of age. She'd been so focused on Steve and Natalie that she hadn't even noticed him until that moment.

"This is my son, David." Natalie's look was one of an adoring mother as she stroked his dark hair from his eyes. "He has a recent spinal cord injury. Steve has been helping him with his therapy by teaching him how to ride."

Catie blinked, her gaze darting from Natalie and David to that big lug who was just standing there, his face three shades brighter. Luckily for her, Catie was rarely at a loss for words. Usually the only one who could do that to her was Jarrod.

She knelt on the ground, at David's level, and extended her hand to him. "Is Steve being nice to you? 'Cause if he's not, I can take him on. Even though he's bigger and older than me, I can still whoop on him."

David grinned as he took Catie's hand and gave her a surprisingly firm handshake. "He's pretty okay." The boy lowered his voice, and added, "Even though I think he's got the hots for my mom."

"David!" Natalie gave her son a playful swat on his shoulder, a mortified look on her pretty face.

Catie laughed and caught her brother's embarrassed expression. "I've never seen you blush before, big guy."

He shook his head and winked at Natalie. "Obviously I don't keep this kid busy enough when I'm there." Steve ruffled David's hair. "Partner, I think you need a few more turns around the corral on Dumpling."

The boy rolled his eyes. "Dumpling is a baby's horse. When can I ride Shadow Warrior?"

Catie stood and dusted off her bare knees. "That's a lot of animal, even for me, and I've been riding since I could walk. I'd hold off a little longer on saddling him up and taking a ride." She placed her hands on her hips and tilted her head. "Now Sassafras would be a good step up. That mare's well trained and gentle as can be. Sass is mine, but I wouldn't mind you riding her when Steve says you're ready."

"Cool!" David's eager gaze shot to Steve. "Can I?"

"Hmmm." Steve rocked back on his heels and stroked his chin with a look of serious consideration. "Not much longer, and I think you'll be ready."

David pumped his small fist in the air. "All right!"

Catie laughed. "I'd better get on back to that bunch over there. If I don't, Dee's likely to tell Jarrod stories about me that I'd rather she keep to herself." She gave David a grin. "Now you make sure you come see me and Sass soon, ya hear?"

A broad smile creased David's face from ear to ear. "You bet!"

As she turned to leave, she lightly punched Steve's biceps. "You and me. We're gonna talk when I get you alone."

He just shook his head and smiled. "Go on and get out of here, Cat."

Cool air chilled her cheeks as she walked toward where Jarrod and the newlyweds were still standing. Boy, when she got home, she was going to have a talk with that brother of hers, and find out why the hell he'd been keeping secret his relationship with Natalie and David Garcia.

As Catie headed back, she passed by a gap between two of the tents. Masculine voices came from behind the tents, piquing her curiosity. She paused, trying to identify them. In the days before Jarrod, she would have taken a peek, just to see if they were good looking or not. Now she could care less.

She shook her head, sure she was losing her mind. All she could think about was one man. Hell, she wasn't even interested in watching anyone else have sex or any of the other kinky things involving multiple partners that she used to fantasize about and thought she'd wanted to try. Compared to sex with Jarrod, that other stuff seemed downright...boring.

Yup. She was losing it.

She started to walk away when she caught a familiar voice saying, "Should'a seen him fuckin' that gal, right below Grand's north range water tower."

Catie stopped in mid-step. Now that was intriguing.

"Think they'll be there Monday night? Maybe we could—"

"Nah. The man's going to be a hair busy."

"Mmm-hmmm. Like to get me a piece of what he had."

"Shut up, dipshit. Keep your mind on what's important. Grand's, Monday, twenty-one hundred hours. Get your ass there early."

"What about Savage?"

"Ah, hell. He's too busy chasing Wilds."

Catie rolled her eyes and walked away. She didn't have time for small town talk. Men always said how women gossiped, but men were just as bad. They just didn't call it gossip.

She'd recognized the first voice, but who had the second one been? Something about him had been familiar, though. A light chill rolled down her spine as a distant memory flashed through her mind.

It couldn't be Reggie Parker. That bastard was long gone. Moved to Texas the last she'd heard, and that was at least eight years ago. There's no way he would have been invited to Dee's reception.

No, Catie thought, *it couldn't have been Reggie.*

While they mingled with the other guests at the reception, it had been all Jarrod could do to not just grab Catie and take her off to a hidden corner in the barn and fuck her ten ways 'til sundown.

As it was, he was forced to perform the social niceties while Catie teased him. Whenever she could get away with it without being noticed by other people, she'd brush her hand over his cock, rub her breasts along his arm, or any number of other taunts that were about to drive him out of his fucking mind.

Come sunset, Jarrod and Catie were sitting with Dee and Jake at one of the tables surrounding the dance floor. The band started up and the newlyweds were dragged out onto the floor to dance a slow one alone before everyone else joined in. Folks with children had headed on home, leaving mostly couples sitting at the tables around the dance floor. Lamps had been arranged to provide romantic lighting and outdoor heaters had been fired up to chase off the early November chill. They'd been lucky that even for Arizona it was warmer than normal this time of year.

While they watched Dee and Jake dance, Jarrod rubbed his fingers along Catie's arm and felt her shiver beneath his touch. Candlelight flickered within the hurricane lamp at the center of the table, the soft glow illuminating her golden features.

"You ready to go, honey?" he said, hoping like hell she'd agree.

"Let's dance first." She moved her lips to his ear and murmured, "Then we can go fuck."

His groin tightened as he slid his hand beneath the tablecloth and eased his fingers up the inside of her thigh, knowing this time he'd reach bare pussy if he kept on going. It was dark, and they were alone at the table, so he wasn't worried about anyone noticing what he was doing. "Sure you want to wait?"

Catie's smile was wicked, and she spread her thighs a little to allow him access. "We haven't done anything naughty here. Yet."

Jarrod's cock burned with need to possess her. His fingers eased up beneath her short skirt, reaching the smooth pussy lips that were already coated with her juices. "Let's get out of here so I can have you for dessert. I can't wait to eat you."

Her eyelashes swept down as his hand cupped her shaved mound. "Just one dance." She moaned as he slipped a finger into her slit and flicked her clit. "Jarrod. Someone might see."

"Maybe you shouldn't have been teasing me all night." He increased his motions, his finger sliding along her slick folds. The way her thighs trembled around his hand, he new she was close to the edge, even though he'd barely touched her. "Open your eyes."

She obeyed and glanced around at the empty tables as he continued to finger her clit. A new song had started, and practically everyone else was on the dance floor. "Oh, God. I'm gonna come."

"That's it." Damn what he would give to take her behind the tent and fuck her now. "Come for me, honey."

The climax scalded Catie in a hot rush and her body jerked against his hand. She bit down on her lip, holding back her cry, and leaned against Jarrod's shoulder, trembling with every stroke of his finger. "Stop." Her voice came out husky as she spotted her friends. "Dee and Jake are coming back."

Jarrod stilled his finger, but kept it in her pussy as the newlyweds returned. She reached down to try to pry his hand away, but he wasn't budging. Her clit continued to throb and pulse, the feeling seeming to amplify as Dee and Jake seated themselves at the table.

"Are you two going to dance?" Dee leaned up against Jake as he brought his arm around her. "Or are you planning to sit here all night?"

"We're—" Catie started just as Jarrod flicked his finger against her sensitized nub, and she damn near came unglued. Furious heat engulfed her and she sat bolt upright while trying to yank Jarrod's finger away from her pussy at the same time. "We were just about to."

She cut Jarrod a glare that said, *just you wait 'til I get you alone.*

He grinned as he removed his hand and pulled down her skirt, then stood. "May I have this dance, honey?"

Jake and Dee exchanged glances that made Catie feel like they knew what Jarrod had been doing to her.

"I'll honey you in a minute," she muttered and took the hand that he offered. His fingers were damp with her juices, and just that made her pussy even wetter than it already was.

Jarrod led her to the edge of the dance floor, where they were in shadow. Even though the band was playing a fairly fast tune, he pulled her close so that their bodies melded together. He rested his hands on her hips, just above her ass while she hooked her hands around his neck and smiled up at him.

Damn but he was handsome. That sexy smile, the way he looked at her like he intended to eat her all up. She loved the feel of his body pressed tight to hers, his cock rigid through his jeans and against her belly. She loved his masculine scent, the way it surrounded her and made her feel content, and loved.

She loved…him.

Oh, God.

A tingling sensation rushed through her as the realization filled her with a strange combination of exhilaration and outright terror. She knew she'd been fighting it all along—but was she ready to face those feelings now?

Jarrod pressed his cheek against hers, his stubble rough against her skin. "I can't wait to get you alone, honey."

"Yeah." She turned her face so that her lips were close to his. "Just kiss me already."

A rumble rose in his chest, reverberating through her as he claimed her mouth. His lips were gentle at first, but then grew hungrier as their bodies continued to sway to the music.

Everything faded around Catie until all she was aware of was the man in her arms, and the knowledge that the impossible had happened.

Catie Wilds had fallen totally, completely, absolutely, in love with Jarrod Savage.

Chapter Eleven

When they finally left the reception, Catie was so horny she could hardly stand it. "Turn here." She pointed to the entrance of a dirt road that led to the mountains behind the Wilds Ranch.

"What do you have in mind?" Jarrod gave her a quick look as he guided the truck down the road she suggested.

In response, she lifted the hem of her blouse, yanked it over her head, and then unclasped her bra and tossed it to the floor. "I'm going to fuck you," she said as she shimmied out of her skirt and kicked off her shoes.

Jarrod groaned and shifted in his seat. "I'm about ready to pull the truck over right here and fuck you in the cab."

Catie knelt on the seat next to him, her naked body pressed tight along his biceps. "Just keep driving 'til I tell you to stop, Sheriff." She rubbed her breasts against his shirt, the material chaffing her sensitive nipples.

He took one hand off the wheel and moved it between her thighs, easing it up to cup her pussy. Moaning, she thrust her hips against his hand. The scent of her juices mingled with his light aftershave and the truck's leather interior.

She nuzzled his neck, drinking in the smell of him. "You should keep hold onto the wheel."

Jarrod flicked his finger against her clit. "I can't keep my hands off you, honey."

"You don't have to wait any longer." She gestured to a cleared area that was a kind of overlook. "Park by those trees."

They'd driven just high enough into the mountains that they could see the glitter of lights from Douglas as well as the Mexican town of Agua Prieta that bordered it to the south.

As soon as Jarrod parked and killed the lights, he grabbed Catie and pulled her onto his lap so that she was straddling him. "I can't wait to be inside you."

Catie moaned as he took one of her nipples into his mouth, and she could hardly speak. "No. Outside. By the tailgate."

His tongue flicked against her other nipple. "It's cold. You'll freeze."

"You'll heat me up." Her voice was low and sensual, and the look that came over his face was positively untamed.

"Hold on." Jarrod yanked the door open. He was so powerful that he was able to grip Catie snug against him with one arm while he climbed out of his truck.

She laughed and clung to him, wrapping her legs tight around his waist. Night air chilled her and caused goose bumps to sprout along her skin. The cool breeze felt erotic brushing across her bare back and ass, while her chest, pussy and thighs were pressed against Jarrod's shirt and jeans.

He strode to the back of the truck and carefully set her down on a clear patch of ground that was pebbly, but didn't hurt her feet.

"Leave your clothes on. Just undo your jeans." She turned her back to him and gripped the tailgate, then pressed her breasts against the cool metal. It felt so good rubbing her nipples across the metal as she waited for Jarrod to free his cock from his jeans. "*Hurry.*"

He chuckled. "You're something else, honey."

Catie looked over her shoulder as he unbuckled his belt and unbuttoned his jeans, just inches away from her. He shoved his pants down around his hips, then pressed his warm cock against her ass.

She held onto the tailgate as she widened her stance and arched her back. "Fuck me now."

Jarrod gently pumped his hips against her ass, his cock rubbing up and down her cheeks. He eased his hands along her slender body, from her slim hips to her small breasts. "I've been dying to do this all night." He moved his cock between her thighs and slid it against her pussy lips.

"Then do it already." Her pussy was drenched, her juices coating his cock as he caressed her folds with it.

He placed the head of his cock at the entrance to her core and gripped her hips tight. With one quick thrust he plunged into her tight entrance, burying himself deep within her. "Damn but it feels good to be inside you."

Catie moaned, enjoying the feel of him inside. He was so long and thick, stretching her, filling her beyond belief. Slowly he moved his cock in and out of her pussy, drawing out the sensations and making her crazy.

"Faster this time, Sheriff." She moved her hips hard against his, trying to bring him deeper inside her.

Jarrod leaned over, covering her back with his warm body while his hips pounded against her ass, his cock thrusting in and out. While he fucked her, he cupped her breasts as he kissed and nipped at her neck.

It was unlikely anyone would happen upon them, but just the thought that someone else could drive up this same road gave Catie the feeling of doing something very naughty. And very exciting.

"You don't know how many times I thought about dragging you into Dee's barn tonight." Jarrod's breathing was harsh as he spoke, his breath warm against her back. "I wanted to take you into the stall and fuck you good and hard."

"Yes." Catie reached between her thighs and fingered her clit. "So good. You fuck me so good."

Jarrod brought one of his hands down and put it over hers, pressing her own fingers tighter into her folds. "I like it when you touch yourself."

All the sensations were too much. The cool air on her naked body, the feel of Jarrod's jeans and shirt scraping her backside, his big cock thrusting in her pussy.

Catie vibrated, the orgasm starting at her scalp and working down her body in a hot flush. This time when she climaxed, she screamed as loud as she could and she barely heard Jarrod's groan as he came.

It felt like every bit of desire for this man came tearing from her lips, hurtling into the night and echoing throughout the valley spread out below.

* * * * *

Come Monday afternoon, Catie was feeling like one of those lovesick airheads that she'd thought were such idiots to lose their hearts over a man. While she straightened up the ranch house she'd actually been *humming*. She couldn't stop thinking about Jarrod. The way it felt to be wrapped tight in his arms. His smell, his taste. The way he kissed her. Made love to her.

Sunday evening he'd brought her back to her ranch after they'd spent the entire day in his home. Touching, feeling, sharing. She'd come close to telling him that she loved him, but somehow she couldn't get the words to come out. A part of her was still afraid that what they had would vanish. That it was about as tangible as smoke and that it would just drift away on the first good wind that swept through.

Yet she knew she could trust him completely — with her life and her heart.

Catie smiled as she undressed and kicked off her moccasins in her bedroom closet, thinking about how exciting it had been to fuck Jarrod while overlooking the distant city lights. She yanked on a pair of jeans, a long-sleeved T-shirt, socks and then boots, preparing to go work in the barn with Sassafras.

On her way out, she grabbed her sheepskin-lined jacket off the coat rack by the door, slipped it on and then headed outside. Overnight the sky had turned dark with clouds that threatened rain, and the nippy air chilled her cheeks.

Steve was in the barn, getting his tack together to take Shadow Warrior out, probably to the Garcia's again.

Sassafras stuck her head over her stall door and whickered at Catie for attention. Catie rubbed Sass's nose while she studied Steve. "When are you going to tell me about what you've been doing with David Garcia? Not to mention Natalie."

Steve shrugged as he took a halter down off the wall and hooked it over a sawhorse by the stall. "Not much to tell."

"Yeah. Right." Catie rolled her eyes. "So, the Garcias are the reason you've been sneaking off every afternoon. And you're just too macho to admit that you're doing something nice and working with this kid, helping him out."

His brown eyes met hers, and the corner of his mouth turned up in a little smile. "He's a neat kid."

She propped both hands on her hips and grinned. "And you've got the hots for his mom."

With another smile, Steve grabbed the saddle blanket off a different sawhorse and put his hand on the door to Shadow Warrior's stall. "Yeah."

"Steve Wilds." Jarrod's voice came loud and clear from the door of the barn slicing through their conversation.

Catie felt a flush of pleasure as she turned toward him, but the chill in his eyes chased away the warmth. "What's wrong?" she asked.

Jarrod's sheriff's star glittered copper in the dim light of the barn as he strode to where she and Steve stood. Deputy Ryan Forrester's expression was unreadable behind his mirrored sunglasses as he followed close behind Jarrod.

"I'm real sorry I have to do this." Jarrod's gaze flicked from Catie to Steve. "Steve Wilds, you're under arrest for suspicion of cattle rustling."

Even as Jarrod spoke, Ryan Forrester held the handcuffs and eased behind Steve. Catie's ears rang, and a ball of acid rolled in her stomach.

"Hold on." Steve dropped the horse blanket and raised his hands in front of him as though holding the men back. "What the hell are you talking about?"

"We've got a lot of evidence." Jarrod's face was stony, his eyes remote and focused only on Steve. "I don't have a choice about this. Everything we've got has you orchestrating the rustling from the get go."

"Are you out of your fucking mind?" Catie clenched her fists at her sides. "There's no way that Steve has had anything to do with it."

"Where's he been every night?" Jarrod's green eyes were cool as they met hers. "Where do you think he got the money for that water heater? And what about that thirty grand in his account?"

"Thirty grand?" Catie repeated, unable to believe she'd heard right.

Steve shook his head. "There's only ten. And I can explain that."

Her gaze swung on Steve as she tried to process what he'd just said. "Ten. Thousand. Dollars." She blinked at him. "Where the hell did you get that kind of money?"

"Like I said, I can explain the ten grand." He turned his attention back to Jarrod. "There's not thirty in the account."

"You're gonna have to come on down and work it out at the county jail." Jarrod sighed and nodded to Ryan.

The deputy began reciting Steve's Miranda rights as he jerked Steve's arms behind his back then cuffed him. While Ryan patted Steve down, his voice droned on like so much background noise.

Catie could only stare, barely hearing the words as the deputy told Steve he had the right to remain silent. Had the right to an attorney. How everything he said could be held against him in a court of law.

"I'm innocent," she heard Steve say to her over the roar in her ears as her eyes met his. "We'll get this straightened out."

"I'll—I'll call a lawyer." She raked her hand through her hair, watching Deputy Forrester escort her brother from the barn. She wanted to scream. Wanted to cry. Wanted to turn to Jarrod, the man she'd thought she'd loved. The man she thought had loved her.

"I'm sorry, honey." Jarrod's voice was low, breaking into her frenzy. "I didn't want to have to do this."

"You bastard." She cut her gaze from the barn door to Jarrod's face. "You used me. You fucked me just so that you could get information on Steve."

His frown deepened. "That's not true and you know it, Catie." He sighed and started to reach for her, like he wanted to comfort her, then dropped his hand at his side. "I've got to go now. We'll talk later."

"Like hell we will." She raised her chin, her vision practically red from her fury. "This is all the talking I'm going to do."

With everything she had, she slammed her fist into his gut.

Her blow caught him by surprise, but he only gritted his teeth as his hand shot out and caught her by the wrist. "You and I, we're not done. I'll be back tonight when I can."

"Fuck you." She jerked her hand and he let it go. "And not literally. Ever again. You and I are through in every goddamn possible way. Just stay the hell away from me, *Sheriff*."

She turned on her boot heel and marched out of the barn and toward the house. Deputy Forrester was waiting beside the Sheriff's Department SUV, but even with his dark glasses on she was sure he was watching her. She saw Steve through the back window of the vehicle, looking straight ahead, his jaw set.

Her knuckles throbbed as she hurried up the stairs, and she felt the heat of Jarrod's gaze on her back. She hoped his gut hurt as much as her hand did. Should have gone for his balls instead.

Catie flung open the screen door and shoved open the door to the house, then slammed it behind her. After locking the door she ripped off her jacket and slung it across the room, wishing she had something big and heavy to throw at Jarrod Savage's head.

The bastard. The never-fucking-her-again *bastard!*

When Catie had calmed down enough that she could talk without screaming, she called Dee to see if her friend could refer a good attorney. Dee was as shocked as Catie at Steve's arrest, and promised to do what she could to help him.

"We all know there's no way he had anything to do with the rustling," Dee said after giving Catie the number of her attorney. "Steve's a good guy."

After calling Janet Jimenez, the attorney, and arranging for the woman to go to the county jail to meet with Steve, Catie hung up and paced the floor of her kitchen, tugging at her earlobe so hard it was a wonder she didn't tear the damn earring out. Her boot steps thunked across the linoleum as she tried to force from her mind thoughts of various methods she could use to kill a certain county sheriff, in a rather painful fashion, and still make it look like an accident.

Catie sighed and shoved her hair out of her face with both hands. *Dammit.* Planning all the ways she could string Jarrod up for using her and breaking her heart wasn't real constructive right now. But it sure felt good.

Instead she needed to concentrate on trying to figure out what to do next, and how to help Steve. Where in the world had he come up with ten *thousand* dollars? Why hadn't he told her?

She braced her hands on the kitchen sink and stared out the window. The late afternoon sun was setting low over the mountains. Not too much longer and it would be dark.

Then it dawned on her. However Steve had gotten that cash, it had to have something to do with Natalie Garcia. That's where he'd been going every day. He'd as good as admitted it in the barn.

Energized by actually doing something towards helping her brother, Catie snatched up her jacket from where she'd thrown it, grabbed her truck key from the hook in the kitchen, bolted out the door and jogged down the steps.

She and Natalie Garcia were gonna have a talk.

After she climbed in and started up the old workhorse of a truck, she gunned the engine and headed as fast as she safely could to the old Karchner place. It had been years since Catie had been there. Her fingers tapped an impatient rhythm against the steering wheel and her thoughts wandered while she drove the beat-up truck the two miles north.

She used to ride Sassafras over to visit Mrs. Karchner, an elderly woman who always had a plate of cookies and a good story to tell about the old days. Not to mention the woman could play a mean game of Scrabble. Catie had never seen much of Old Man Karchner. Even though he'd been in his late seventies back then, he'd always been out working in his garden, and never did have anything to say the times she did run across him. One of those strong, silent types, she supposed.

When Mrs. Karchner passed away, Catie had been devastated. She still missed the old woman. Her stomach clenched as she remembered the woman's lilac perfume and the home's comforting smells of fresh baked cookies and hot apple pie. Mrs. Karchner had been more like a mom to Catie than any of the number of wives her father had brought through her own home. And her 'real' mother…well, it'd been years since Catie had seen her. She didn't even know if the woman was alive any longer.

Natalie Garcia was in the front yard when Catie drove up. The woman had on a pair of work gloves, and she was pruning one of the weeping willow trees in the front yard. Out near the barn in the backyard, Catie saw David in his wheelchair playing with a golden retriever.

While Catie climbed out of the truck, Natalie tossed the pruning sheers onto the dead grass at her feet. She shucked off her gloves, leaving them with the garden tool before walking up to Catie. A smile lit Natalie's face until she got a good look at Catie's expression.

"Steve?" Natalie's hand went to her heart as if trying to calm it. "Did something happen to him? Is he all right?"

Catie shoved her hands in her front pockets. "He's been arrested."

"What?" Shock registered on the woman's face, her palm going from her chest to her mouth. "Why?"

"That's what I'm trying to figure out." Catie explained what Jarrod had said when he'd arrested Steve. "It sounds like the biggest thing they've got is a shitload of money deposited into his account."

Natalie took a deep breath and pushed her black hair off her forehead with one hand. "The ten thousand I can tell you about, and it's perfectly legal. It's a lump sum grant. Payment." She gestured toward the barn where David was laughing and doing wheelies in his wheelchair. "A private organization provided the grant for my son to have extensive therapy to help him rehabilitate after his spinal cord injury. I signed a contract with your brother to work with David."

Catie tilted her head. "You hired my brother?"

"He's been my son's companion for a couple of months now, taking him on horseback rides every afternoon." The woman gave a quick smile. "Steve plans to start a full time therapeutic horseback program for kids with CP and spinal cord injuries."

"And every evening…" Catie let her voice trail off as she studied Natalie.

A flush stole over Natalie's face. "When I get David settled down for the night, Steve and I do spend time together." She gestured with one hand toward Douglas. "Sometimes *mi madre* comes to watch David while Steve and I go out."

Okay, after she did away with Jarrod, Catie was going to kill her big brother. Nothing like keeping his entire life secret from his little sister. *The jerk.*

At Catie's frown, Natalie's face fell. "You don't approve, do you," she said, a statement, not a question.

"It's not that." Catie shook her head. "I just don't understand why he kept this all secret from me."

"Steve has a hard time opening up." Natalie sighed and gave a wry smile. "He's a hard man to get anything out of, but once we reached a certain point in our relationship we both began sharing our dreams."

Catie felt like she'd been kicked in the gut. She was Steve's sister, yet she'd never taken the time to find out if he had any dreams beyond trying to make the ranch productive. She sighed. "All right. So Steve has a secret life he didn't bother to tell me about. But that doesn't explain the other twenty grand in his account."

"Steve would never do anything illegal." Natalie pursed her lips, and then shook her head. "I'd better go call *mi madre* to see if she can watch David." She scooped up the gloves and pruning sheers. "I've got all the grant paperwork for the ten thousand, and the contract and payment agreements. Even the plans for the riding program. I'll take it all down to the county jail. And I've got to tell them that he's been with me until late, just about every single night."

Catie quirked a brow. "Sounds like the two of you had some fun."

Natalie gave Catie a smile. "We found whatever time and whatever place we could, to be alone."

"Should'a seen him fuckin' that gal, right below Grand's north range water tower."

Catie frowned as the memory popped into her mind—the words she'd overheard at the reception. "Did you and Steve, ah, have sex under Kev Grand's water tower?"

Embarrassment covered Natalie's pretty face. "Somebody saw us?"

But another wheel clicked in Catie's mind as she thought back to the rest of the conversation between the two men—

"Think they'll be there Monday night? Maybe we could — "

"Nah. The man's going to be a hair busy."

"Mmm-hmmm. Like to get me a piece of what he had."

"Shut up, dipshit. Keep your mind on what's important. Grand's, Monday, twenty-one hundred hours. Get your ass there early."

"One more thing." Catie's gaze met Natalie's. "I need to know the time. Was it around nine at night?"

"Yes." Natalie nodded and released a sigh. "I can't believe someone saw us out in the field. There was nothing but cows." Her eyes widened. "Unless someone was out in the mesquite bushes, or up on Catwalk Trail."

Catie tried to give Natalie a smile, but it felt more like a grimace. "I know that was a real personal question to ask, but I had to know."

After saying goodbye to Natalie, Catie drove back to her ranch, puzzling out the significance of what those men had said at Dee and Jake's reception.

And what it all had to do with her brother and cattle rustling.

Chapter Twelve

By the time Catie arrived home, it was dark and she had everything worked out in her mind. She knew exactly what she needed to do and how she'd go about it.

Catie prepared with single-minded determination, putting on her tennis shoes rather than her boots. They'd be quieter and it would be easier to run if she had to. She slipped her pocketknife into the front pocket of her jeans. As far as she was concerned, it was up to her to clear her brother's name and prove who the real culprits were.

The men she'd overheard at the MacLeod-Reynolds barbeque had said they were planning to meet at twenty-one hundred hours Monday night. That would be nine tonight. And it was at the same location where they'd seen Steve and Natalie fuck, because the second man had hoped they'd be there again so he could watch.

At Kev Grand's water tower in his north pasture.

No wonder the son-of-a-bitch knew Steve would be busy tonight. He'd known Steve would be arrested, likely because he'd planted it himself.

What about Savage?

Ah, hell. He's too busy chasing Wilds.

The bastards hadn't been talking about Jarrod chasing Catie, they'd been talking about Jarrod following the false leads on Steve.

It was about eight o'clock when she snatched up the cordless, prepared to call Jarrod. She stopped just as she started to dial, and stared at the phone. Why should she call him? He was the asshole who'd arrested her brother. After all, considering who it was she'd overheard, Jarrod very well could be a part of the whole damn mess. And look at how he'd used her. Fucked her to get information on Steve.

Even though her mind and heart wanted to reject that thought, right now she didn't feel like she could trust anyone.

The piercing wail of the phone bolted through Catie and she almost dropped the cordless. Her heart pounded as she checked the display. Dee's number. Thank God.

Catie pressed the *on* button and brought the phone to her ear. "What's up?"

"Just calling to see how you're holding up." Dee paused, her voice filled with concern. "And to check on how Steve's doing."

"I'm fine. And Steve—how good could he be doing when he's in jail on bullshit charges?" Catie sighed and gripped the phone tighter. "Listen. I'm going to go check something out. I think I know who has been doing all this rustling."

"What? Who?" Dee's voice rose. "You're not about to go off and do anything dangerous, are you?"

"I'm just going to take Sass out to Kev Grand's north range, near his water tower." Catie pushed her hand away from her face as she spoke. "I can go up around back on Catwalk Trail. I'll tether Sass in the trees, and then get a little closer to see what's going on."

"That's too dangerous." Dee's tone was firm. "Call the Sheriff's Department."

"No fucking way." Catie knew that her friend was only concerned for her, but she couldn't help but feel the twist of anger in her gut. Jarrod. The bastard. The using son of a bitch. "I can't go to the law. It's the Sheriff's Department that I'm worried about. I'm going to the meeting place. I'll stay out of sight and just get some information so that I have something to take to the authorities. Something that Jarrod can't ignore."

"Dammit, Catie, it's way too dangerous," Dee insisted. Catie could easily picture her friend's concerned expression. "Jake is working late on a drug bust. He should be home any moment and he can go."

Catie glanced up at the kitchen clock. "Won't be soon enough. They're meeting in about fifty minutes. I've got just enough time to saddle up Sass and get over there and find a good hiding place.

"*No.*"

"I'll call you when I get back."

"Dammit, Catie."

"Bye." Catie tossed the cordless on the counter and checked the clock again. She'd better get her ass in gear and get out to Grand's north range.

* * * * *

Jarrod rubbed his hand over his stubbled cheeks as he strode into his home and slammed the door behind him. It had been one hell of a day.

In his gut he knew Steve Wilds was innocent, but the setup had been good. Of course there was the large amount of cash deposited into Wilds' account. But the most damning evidence had been found in the cabin behind the Wilds Ranch. The same one where Jarrod had fingered Catie while she watched that trio fuck.

Jarrod tossed his Stetson on the back of a couch and strode toward the kitchen to fix himself dinner as he mulled over the case. In the Wilds' cabin, Jarrod and Forrester had discovered rustling plans, along with lists of ranches that had been hit over the last two months. Lists that had broken down exactly how many cattle had been stolen. Detailed income reports that had shown the cattle being sold to unnamed buyers for a sum greater than twenty grand.

Steve's name had been written all over every damn document.

Jarrod blew out his breath in a hard rush as he grabbed sandwich makings out of the fridge. As far as he was concerned, Steve Wilds had been royally framed. And Jarrod had a pretty good idea who'd done the framing. He just had to prove it.

But first he needed to eat, and then go talk some sense into Catie Wilds.

Just as Jarrod finished making his turkey and rye sandwich, the phone rang. He shoved the mayo into the fridge while grabbing the handset off the wall.

"Savage here."

"Sheriff, this is Dee MacLeod-Reynolds." The urgency in her voice told him something was seriously wrong.

"What's happened?"

"Nothing. Yet. It's just that Catie's gone off and I'm afraid she's going to get herself in some trouble."

Jarrod's heart thudded at the thought of something happening to Catie. "Details. Now."

Dee explained what Catie had said, and the trail she was using to get there. "She was in a rush. Something about getting to the water tower before nine so she could find a good spot to hide."

"The little idiot." Jarrod clenched his jaw. "See if you can get Jake out there. I'll head out without back-up. Can't go into details."

"All right. Hurry, Jarrod."

He punched off the phone and tossed it on the counter, and scooped up his sandwich, figuring he could eat it on the way and knowing he needed the fuel to think clearly. He still had on his utility belt, firearm and bulletproof vest. After grabbing his hat, he strode out the door.

* * * * *

Sassafras whickered as she picked her way along Catwalk Trail behind Kev Grand's northern range. "Shhh." Catie patted the mare's neck. "We need to be extra quiet, girl."

The horse tossed her head like she understood. The only sounds in the night were the creak of saddle leather, Sass's horseshoes clonking against small rocks on the trail and the yelp of coyotes in the distance. The scents of piñon, juniper and horse met her nose.

Catie leaned low in the saddle, trying to peer at the water tower through the brush at the same time. A full moon hung low in the sky, giving a little light to see by whenever it wasn't hidden by clouds. She saw nothing but cattle and cacti, so with any luck she'd beaten the bastards to their meeting place.

When she was still far enough away that she could safely leave Sass, Catie dismounted and tethered the mare to a paloverde tree. The crunch of rocks beneath her tennis shoes seemed loud in the night, even as she tried to step quietly down the trail. About a hundred feet from the water tower, she crouched behind the last remaining boulders before the rangeland. The boulders were large, and she was small enough that she didn't think she'd have a problem staying out of sight.

It had to be getting close to nine. Her heart pounded and her mouth grew dry as she heard the rumble of tires on the dirt road leading to the water tower, and the low roar of an engine. Headlights sliced through the darkness, becoming brighter and brighter as the sound of the vehicle grew louder along with a rattling noise, as if the truck was pulling some kind of trailer.

The vehicle's brakes squealed and its tires slid in the dirt as the truck came to a stop. The engine cut off and the lights went out. Catie tugged at her ear while trying to slow her breathing as she forced herself to remain behind the boulder and not look to see who it was. She needed to wait just a moment longer.

The sound of first one door slamming and then another met her ears, and she took a deep breath. Two men. It had to be both of them. She rubbed her sweaty palms on her jeans and slowly peeked over the boulders.

A one-ton truck was parked maybe fifty feet from where she was hidden. Behind the truck was an enormous stock trailer. A couple of men in baseball caps walked around toward the back of the trailer, and one man stood at the front of the truck as he lit a cigarette. The small flame of the lighter lit up his features for a second, and then he turned and sauntered toward the stock trailer.

Catie's gut churned as she recognized the bastard. She'd know that arrogant jaw, those deep set eyes and that swagger anywhere. Her skin prickled and a hot rush of anger flooded her from head to toe. The other voice she'd heard at the barbeque, the one she hadn't been sure of but had wondered—she'd been right. It *was* Reggie Parker. That bastard who'd tried to rape her when she was in high school.

While she tried to calm her fury, she crouched on her knees, out of sight, and pressed her forehead against the cool boulder. Thank God Steve had heard about Reggie bragging to his friends that he planned to score with her at the drive-in. She'd been fortunate enough that all he'd managed to do was pop a couple buttons off her blouse before Steve had arrived and beat the holy living shit out of him. Reggie's pawing had been enough to scare her off of dating for awhile, but as she grew older she learned how to separate the assholes from the good guys.

Now that Reggie was back from Texas, he probably thought of this as some twisted form of revenge—framing Steve for the cattle rustling. And that comment she'd overheard, about getting a piece of what Steve had…she knew now he'd been referring to Natalie. No doubt it was another twisted way he'd be getting even with Steve.

Catie took a deep breath, her forehead still against the boulder, while she tried to decide what to do next. Maybe she'd get the chance to settle the score for what had been done to her big brother. And instead of Reggie's ass, she'd kick him in the balls so hard he'd be singing falsetto in the St. Jude's Boy's Choir for the rest of his miserable life.

The trick now was figuring out how to get close enough to permanently damage the man's family jewels—and not get herself killed in the process.

A click by Catie's ear sent ice shooting through her veins. The cool metal of a gun barrel slid along her cheek, telling her all she needed to know.

She was in deep shit.

* * * * *

Once he got on the road, Jarrod made the ten mile drive to Kev Grand's ranch in about eight minutes flat. Problem was, he had to park a good quarter mile away, just to make sure he didn't alert the bastards to his presence.

By the time he reached the water tower, it was at least a quarter past nine, the time Catie had apparently thought the rendezvous was supposed to be. He eased through the mesquite bushes and brush, blood thrumming in his veins, until he spotted the water tower. Moonlight had grown bright enough that he could easily make out a large cattle trailer parked behind a good sized truck near the tower.

But what caught his attention were the men herding cattle into the trailer. One man dogged the beasts by horseback while three other bastards were on foot, using cattle prods to get the animals into the trailer. The men's shouts and whistles along with the low of cattle filled the night. They were at least a couple of miles from the nearest ranch house, so likely they had no real concern they'd be heard.

According to Dee's directions, Catwalk Trail was to the right of where he was crouched. Jarrod started to work his way toward the trail when hair prickled at his nape. Someone was coming up behind him.

In one smooth movement he whirled while drawing his gun, at the same time keeping in a crouch.

"Savage." A low voice came from the darkness. "It's me. Jake Reynolds."

Jarrod's muscles relaxed and he lowered his weapon. "Thanks for joining the fun." He re-holstered his gun and nodded toward the rustlers as Reynolds moved closer and crouched beside him. "Not sure where Catie is, but it looks like she was right."

Reynolds clenched his jaw. "I'll bet these sons-of-a-bitches took Dee's cattle."

Jarrod nodded as he watched the men rounding up the herd. "And everyone else's."

"Steve Wilds was framed, wasn't he?" Reynolds asked quietly.

"That's been my gut feeling." Jarrod shifted his position while keeping his eyes on the rustlers.

"Recognize any of 'em?"

"Hard to tell from here." Jarrod clenched his fist, imagining the pleasure he'd take in knocking the crap out of the SOB he was sure was responsible. "I'd bet a year's salary that I know the bastard on horseback."

"They're finished loading the trailer," Reynolds said as the rustlers slammed the gate behind the last cow they'd loaded. "You and I can take them."

"Yeah." Jarrod nodded, his mouth set in a grim line. "But first I've got to make sure Catie's safe."

"Take care of your woman." The expression on Reynolds' face said he'd do the same thing if he was in Jarrod's shoes. "Dee was sure Catie would be on Catwalk Trail." Reynolds gestured in the direction Jarrod had been about to head earlier.

"I'll check there first." Jarrod started forward when a furious shriek cut through the sounds of the cattle and men's voices.

A woman.

Catie.

* * * * *

The thieves left Catie alone as they loaded up the trailer. She was sitting on the ground, her back against the truck tire, her hands bound in her lap. While they were busy stealing cattle, Catie managed to work the pocketknife up and out of her pocket.

During the slow process, she had plenty of time to think about everything. She knew now that Jarrod had only been doing his job. Obviously the bastards had framed her brother, and if Jarrod hadn't taken Steve in, then it would have looked like he was playing favors.

Catie finally opened the damn pocketknife when Reggie Parker walked up. She barely had time to hide the knife in her cupped palms, and she only hoped he hadn't seen the metal glinting in the moonlight.

"Touch me and die, *bastard*," Catie told Reggie, her face twisted in a murderous scowl.

"Wild little thing, aren't you?" Parker laughed and ambled closer, that arrogant look on his face. It galled Catie to remember that she'd thought he was handsome in high school. "We've got a bit of lost time to make up for, hon."

She narrowed her eyes. All right. Her legs hadn't been bound, so she could kick the shit out of him. Just let him come closer and she'd make him wish he hadn't shown up tonight.

"Load the bitch up and let's get the hell out of here." Ryan Forrester guided his horse closer to where Reggie was eyeing Catie. "You can have your fun when we get this shipment to El Paso."

"You're a sneaky bastard, aren't you?" Catie glared at Ryan. "Framing my brother, making sure the Sheriff's Department was always following some false lead you'd planted while you've been laughing your ass off."

Reggie chuckled and cut in, "I kinda liked how we made it look like it was that fucker Wilds who was trying to swipe the MacLeod bull. Used an appaloosa just like the one you own." His smile turned to a frown. "Damn that Lawless. Kept us from nabbing that pricey bull."

Catie narrowed her eyes at Ryan. "Planting that twenty grand in Steve's account to really make things look bad for him was just swell of you."

Ryan shrugged. "Business is business, sugar. I've got bills and working for the county doesn't pay for shit."

"Ah, this ain't nuthin'." Reggie Parker slicked his hair back with one hand while his gaze raked over Catie. "This's just been a cover for the real money."

"Shut up, asshole." Forrester scowled at Reggie. "Let's get the hell out of here." The deputy turned his horse toward the other two men who were standing at the back of the truck, men that Catie hadn't recognized.

Reggie walked up to her and grinned. "This is gonna be fun." He leaned over to grab Catie by her upper arms and she could smell the stench of cigarettes and alcohol on his breath.

As he started to touch her, Catie drew her knee up and shot out her foot. At the same time she screamed with the force of her fury, and slammed her foot into the man's kneecap with all the power she possessed. "Bastard," she shouted. "That's for Steve."

A sickening pop traveled from the sole of her shoe and up her leg as his knee buckled. Reggie shrieked and dropped the ground, landing flat on his ass. At the same moment she clenched the handle of the pocketknife with both bound hands and launched her body at him, driving the knife through the thick leather of his boot as she came down, and drilling the blade into his foot. He screamed again.

"That was for me," she shouted. "Teach you to mess with me or my brother, you son-of-a-bitch." She'd landed on her belly, her hands still around the knife hilt, her face close to the foot she'd just impaled.

"Bitch!" Reggie's face was contorted with pain, a sheen of sweat glossing is forehead, glittering strangely in the moonlight. "Forrester. The bitch stabbed me. And she fucked up my knee."

Reggie yanked a gun out of his back pocket and pointed it at her, his hands trembling and sweat rolling down his face. "You're gonna pay, you goddamn whore."

Catie felt blood draining from her face as she stared down the barrel of the gun that shook from the force of his trembling—a mere foot from her face.

Oh, shit. I'm going to die.

Just as she expected to feel a bullet slam into her, a shot exploded in the night, so loud Catie's ears rang. At the same moment the gun flew from Reggie's hand.

And then it was chaos.

Jarrod whipped around the truck, his gun pointed right at Reggie. "Move a muscle and die."

At the same moment Jake Reynolds shouted, "You're under arrest," and knocked one of the men to the ground.

Ryan Forrester wheeled his horse around and bolted into the darkness, and the fourth man took off running in the opposite direction.

"Fuck." Jarrod kept his gun trained on Reggie as he grabbed the handcuffs from his belt. "Please. Just give me an excuse to wipe you off the face of this planet, you son-of-a-bitch."

Fear, relief, fury, love—every emotion cycled through Catie like a tornado as she watched Jarrod and the scene unfolding before her.

Catie scrambled away from Reggie, leaving the knife in his boot. She saw that Jake had the other man cuffed and facedown in the dirt. "Looks like we've got help," Jake said as he gestured toward Catwalk Trail.

Squinting, Catie peered into moonlit night and saw that the third man was being marched back towards them at gunpoint—and Jess Lawless was the man behind the gun.

"Nice of you join us, Lawless," Jarrod said as he cuffed Reggie. "Don't suppose you managed to get Forrester while you were at it?"

Jess offered a tight smile. "No, but I will."

One-handed, Jarrod grabbed Reggie by the front of his shirt and hauled him up to stand. Reggie's face was white and trembling, and he was obviously in pain from the damage Catie had inflicted.

"Consider yourself lucky that Catie got a hold of you before I did." Jarrod brought Reggie's face close to his. Jarrod's eyes and expression were absolutely furious—

Catie had never seen him so angry. "If you ever touch my woman again, I'll kill you, you miserable bastard."

Jarrod shoved Reggie away from him, and the man went sprawling flat on his back, shrieking out in obvious pain.

In one quick movement, Jarrod turned and scooped Catie up from the ground, holding her so tight she could hardly breathe. "Dammit, you little shit. Don't you ever scare me like that again."

He never gave her a chance to respond. He kissed her face, her hair, her nose and then her mouth. A hard, passionate, feral kiss that seared through Catie like wildfire.

When he finally raised his head he looked down at her with so much caring and love she couldn't think straight. "I don't give a shit what you think. You and I are getting married. And the sooner the better, 'cause I damn sure need to keep an eye on you."

Catie blinked as what he'd said sank in. A warm feeling spread through her, a feeling like nothing she'd ever known before. She licked her lips, and then smiled. "All right." At the look of satisfaction on his face, she added, "But only so I can keep an eye on you, too, Sheriff."

After Jarrod had made sure Catie was safe, her bonds removed, and all the prisoners subdued, he took Jess and Jake aside.

"You're not really a ranch foreman, are you, Lawless?" Jarrod said as he studied the man's eyes.

Reynolds folded his arms and leaned back as though to watch the show. "I've had suspicions myself, since I met you."

"You're right." Lawless' mouth quirked into a slight grimace. He glanced to where Catie was sitting, like he wanted to make sure she couldn't hear. "I'm deep undercover. Special Agent Jesse Lawless with the DEA. I'll show you my badge later on."

Jarrod pushed the brim of his hat up. "Tell us about it."

"We've been after Forrester for sometime." Lawless jerked his head in the direction the man had ridden off. "He got himself involved with the Mexican drug cartel trying to pay off heavy gambling debts. From the intelligence we've gathered, this whole rustling scheme was designed to keep the focus off what's really going on. A big drug deal is going down around here, and soon. Real soon."

Heated anger rushed through Jarrod. "Why the hell wasn't I notified about any of this?"

"I'd like to know the answer, too." Reynolds set his jaw. "Customs should have been in on this from the start."

"I agree," Jess replied. "But we couldn't be sure that no one else in the Sheriff's Department was involved, or in any of the law enforcement branches here for that matter. That's part of my job—to sort out the good guys from the bad guys."

Jess' gaze cut to Catie who was walking toward them. "But this stays with the three of us. You're not to tell *anyone* else."

Jarrod nodded and left the men, striding toward Catie. Her blonde hair was mussed, dirt streaked across her face, her clothes were rumpled and dirty—she'd never looked more beautiful

When he reached her, he clamped his hands around her tiny waist and swooped her into his arms. She laughed and wrapped her legs around his waist, grabbed his cheeks and planted a kiss on his lips.

"Come on, Sheriff." She cupped his face in her hands. "Let's go home."

Chapter Thirteen

I must be out of my mind, Catie thought as Jarrod led her from his vehicle. She was blindfolded, her hands tied securely behind her back with a silk scarf. He held her close, his arm draped around her shoulders as he guided her forward. *Yeah. Out of my mind in love.*

She could hardly believe that she was now Catie Savage. She'd thought about keeping her maiden name, like Dee had done, but Catie Wilds-Savage sounded like the name of a bad porn star. It had been a week since they'd captured the rustlers, and Jarrod insisted he couldn't wait any longer. Hell, neither could she.

Jarrod and Catie had been married just an hour ago at the Bisbee City Hall by the Justice of the Peace. Dee and Jake had been in attendance, along with Jess Lawless, not to mention Steve, Natalie and her son David. Catie had an idea that Steve might be heading down the aisle real soon himself.

Being blindfolded heightened every one of her senses. A car passed in the distance and a small dog yapped somewhere nearby. Beneath her heels she felt asphalt then sidewalk as Jarrod helped her along. A gentle wind stirred the short hair against her neck, the chill air carrying the fragrance of fall and holidays just around the corner.

Catie's skin tingled with absolute awareness of the man with her, his muscled arm holding her secure. The light scent of his aftershave enveloped her, along with his own unique masculine smell. Even blindfolded in a roomful of men, she'd know his elemental scent, the taste of his skin, the feel of his hard body against hers.

"I can't believe I let you do this to me." Catie lifted her head and tried to peek beneath the blindfold, but the black scarf was too well wrapped around her eyes. "Now that we're here, why don't you tell me where we are and what we're doing?"

Jarrod laughed, his husky chuckle shooting a fireball straight through her belly to her pussy. "Be careful. In about two more steps we're gonna head up a set of stairs."

Her feet faltered and Jarrod murmured, "What the hell," and then the next thing she knew his arms were around her waist and he was raising her up and throwing her over his shoulder.

"Jarrod!" she cried out and laughed all at once as blood rushed to her head and she felt his body move beneath her as he climbed the stairs. The necklace of linked gold hearts and diamonds slid up over her chin, probably making her look even more ridiculous. She wished her hands weren't bound so that she could pound on him or something.

Her wedding dress was an ocean blue silky affair that only reached the top of her thighs. She'd loved how it looked on her, and by the way Jarrod had eyed her all morning, she knew he liked it, too.

"Let me down. Someone's gonna see up my dress." And they'd get one hell of a view, since as usual she wasn't wearing any underwear.

His boots clomped up the wooden steps as he smoothed down her silky skirt, holding his arm tight under her ass. "Quiet down, woman."

"You know you're going to pay for this, don't you?" She sank her teeth into his western dress shirt and the firm skin beneath it, giving him a playful bite.

"Hey." Jarrod shrugged beneath her mouth and swatted her ass. "Watch it, wildcat." He reached a landing, the hollow sound of wood beneath his boots as he started across it. "Or I'm gonna have to teach you a lesson."

"Ha." The squeak of a screen door met her ears, and a rush of warm air washed over her as he stepped onto a throw rug or flooring that must have been carpeted since his boot steps were now muffled. She caught a potpourri of smells—warm bread, cinnamon, and spices. "You can let me go now."

He shifted her in his arms, his grip tighter than ever. "Pipe down."

Before she had a chance to tell him off, a woman laughed and said, "Welcome to Nicole's Bed-and-Breakfast, Sheriff Savage. And that must be your bride?"

"Good to see you again." Jarrod swatted Catie's butt a second time, and she gasped from the contact. "Catie, meet Nicole."

Heat rushed through Catie from the tips of her toes to the ends of the hair that was hanging in her face. How embarrassing. Some strange woman could see her butt sticking up in the air, and she was blindfolded and trussed up like a roped calf at a rodeo.

"Hi," Catie muttered. "Can you knock this guy over the head with a shovel or something? I'd appreciate it."

"I'll see what I can do." Humor infused Nicole's pleasant voice. "Here's your key, Sheriff. I reserved the best room we have to offer. Just head up those stairs, then down the hall and it's the last door on the left."

"Thank you kindly," the big oaf replied and Catie's head spun as he turned. His boots thumped against wood flooring again.

"You are *so* dead, Jarrod Savage," Catie muttered as he climbed another set of stairs and she bounced against his back. "Right after I fuck you, I'm gonna kill you."

He chuckled, the deep sound reverberation from his body and straight through her. "You'll be too worn out once I get through with you, honey."

Jarrod's cock throbbed as he slid the key into the lock and opened the door to the room. The woman over his shoulder was going to get the biggest fucking of her life. After he shut and locked the door behind him, he strode across the hardwood floor to the curtained four-poster bed, and sat down on the mattress.

He carefully swung Catie from his shoulder and laid her face down across his lap, her belly across his thighs, her wrists still tied securely behind her back.

His wife. Catie was now his wife, and he couldn't be a prouder man.

"Untie me and take off this blindfold." Her voice was muffled. "I can't wait to get my hands on you."

"You'll just have to wait a little longer, honey." He adjusted her across his lap so that her ass was sticking practically straight up. "If you don't behave, I'll have to gag you, too."

"Jarrod—" she started, but when he pushed her skirt up over her bare butt, the threat in her voice turned into a moan.

"Damn you have a beautiful ass." He placed his palms on the smooth cheeks and squeezed. "After that stunt you pulled last week and almost getting yourself killed, I think you need to be punished real good."

"You're not going to spank me, are you?" Catie sounded both worried and aroused. Definitely aroused.

"I kept warning you that I'd have to if you didn't behave." Jarrod swatted her ass and Catie gasped. "And you were a bad girl, honey."

"Jarrod." Her voice was hoarse as she wiggled her butt and squirmed on his lap, her belly rubbing against his cock. "How bad was I?"

"Real bad." Jarrod grinned rubbing his calloused fingers over the slightly reddened flesh. He swatted her again and her moan made him ache to fuck her now. Hard and fast.

Instead he slid his fingers down her crack and between her thighs to the shaved lips of her pussy, and she spread her legs a little, giving him better access. The scent of Catie's juices mingled with her vanilla musk scent, and he had to taste her.

"Please…" She groaned as he dipped his fingers into her creamy heat.

"Damn but you're wet." Jarrod moved his fingers within her folds, then thrust them into her core. "But you still need to be punished before I can fuck you."

"*Jarrod.*" She gasped and pushed her hips against his hand.

He drew his fingers out of her pussy and brought them to his mouth, tasting her juices before delving back into her wetness. When his fingers were slick again, he trailed them over her crack to her cheeks, smoothing her fluids over her. And then swatted the flat of his hand against her ass again.

Catie cried out, damn near climaxing when he spanked her. Her ass tingled, thighs trembled and abs tightened, her clit so stimulated that one touch would send her over.

The man was about to drive her out of her mind. She never realized how much of a turn-on being tied up, blindfolded, and spanked would be. It felt unbelievably erotic lying across Jarrod's lap, her skirt up to her hips and her ass bared to him.

"Are you going to be a good girl now?" He rubbed his hand over the cheeks that still stung from that last swat.

"Bastard," she muttered, and then gasped as he spanked her again.

"Do you need another reminder?" His voice thrummed with arousal, his cock hard through his slacks and pressing against her belly, and she knew he was as horny as she was. "Or are you going to apologize for misbehaving?"

"Why should I—" Her words died in her throat as he swatted her. Oh, God, she had to come. She was so damn close.

"Well?" Jarrod rubbed her ass cheeks then moved his hand down to cup her mound and just held it there.

The bastard. He knew what he was doing to her.

Catie swallowed. "I—I'm sorry."

He cupped his hand tighter around her pussy, but didn't do anything more, didn't do what she needed him to. "And?"

"I promise I'll be good." Catie squirmed on his lap. "Just make me come, Jarrod. *Please.'*

Jarrod slapped her ass again, the stinging sensation going straight to her pussy. Even as she cried out, he slipped a couple of fingers into her folds and thrust into her core, fucking her with his fingers. "Damn but you feel good. I've got to have you around my cock."

"Yes." Catie's thoughts whirled, her body so close to the edge. Jarrod flicked her clit with his thumb, and all it took was one time to send her straight over the cliff.

She shrieked and clenched her thighs tight around his hand, her body jerking against his thighs. A dizzy sensation swirled through her, magnified by being upside down for so long.

Some part of her recognized that Jarrod was removing the scarf that bound her hands. Her pussy continued to throb from her orgasm as he massaged her wrists, and then she felt him tugging on the tie to the scarf around her eyes and freeing it before rolling her over and cradling her in his arms. Her heart necklace slid back down around her neck, feeling cool against her skin.

Catie blinked up at the incredibly handsome man that held her tight. "I owe you, big guy," she murmured.

"Oh?" His slow sexy grin sent more tingles to her pussy. "Do I need to spank you again?"

She moved her hand up to his face and cupped his cheek, rubbing her palm against his stubble. "It's my turn, Sheriff."

"Uh, no." He shook his head. "I can't say that I'd let you spank me."

Catie smiled. "That's not what I had in mind. Now let me up."

Jarrod slid her off his lap and helped her to stand on the bisque-colored throw rug beside the bed, her skirt settling back down over her ass. He moved behind her and rubbed her shoulders and arms, probably realizing that they ached from having her hands tied behind her back for so long. She sighed and leaned against him, enjoying the feel of his strong fingers working her muscles.

"This room is beautiful." Her gaze moved from the antique dresser and chest of drawers to the four poster bed complete with curtains in a rich shade of cream. Long twisted silk ropes, complete with tassels, tied back the curtains. "Where did you find this place?"

"A friend recommended it." The heat of his palms burned through her light blouse as he massaged her and she shivered as he moved his lips to her hair. "From what I was told, Nicole moved to Bisbee from Douglas a year ago when she inherited this place from a relative. She turned it into a small bed-and-breakfast."

Catie turned in Jarrod's arms, slid her hands up his shirt and linked her fingers behind his neck. "I like it." With an impish grin she moved one hand up to his Stetson and pushed it off his head so that it landed on the floor with a soft thunk. "But right now all I want to do is fuck you on that gorgeous bed."

Jarrod's eyes were dark and heavy-lidded with desire. "I certainly hate to keep a lady waiting."

He started to bring his lips to hers, but Catie put her palm over his mouth. "You had your fun. Now it's my turn."

Jarrod raised an eyebrow, wondering what his little wildcat was up to. He wanted her so bad it was all he could do to hold himself from throwing her on that bed, yank his cock out of his slacks, push up her dress, and thrust into her wet pussy.

Her palm was soft against his lips, and he brought his hand to hers, holding it tight as he stroked his tongue against the soft skin.

Catie groaned, her eyelids fluttering. She placed her other hand against his chest and pushed. "Fair's fair, Sheriff Savage."

He smiled and released her, but clenched his jaw as she pulled open the snaps of his dress shirt then rubbed her palms up his bare chest, an intent expression on her face. She pushed the shirt away from his shoulders, eased it off his arms, and tossed it to the side.

The smile on her face was wickedly erotic as she leaned forward and licked his nipple. Jarrod sucked in his breath at the feel of her wet tongue flicking across the tight nub and the sprinkling of hair around it. Her hands continued to explore him, stroking his chest and abs, down to the waistband of his slacks and back up again. She moved her mouth to his other nipple, giving it the same treatment, drawing out his torture.

Jarrod leaned his head back and groaned as he brought his hands up to Catie's slim hips and cupped her ass, pressing her tight to his erection.

"Not so fast, mister." She trailed lazy strokes with her tongue down his chest, pushing her butt back against his hands.

He sucked in his breath as she nipped at the skin around his belly button, then flicked her tongue inside. The sensual feeling added fuel to his hunger for her, and he clenched his hands in the soft material of her skirt.

"Ah-ah-ah." Catie's hands moved to his belt buckle as she looked up, her chocolate eyes meeting his. "Get your paws off."

"Don't mess with me, woman," he practically growled at her. He felt raw and wild, ready to fuck her like an untamed beast.

"Behave." She undid his belt buckle and then unbuttoned his fly, her knuckles brushing his erection as she worked the zipper down. His cock jerked against her touch and a naughty smile curved her lips.

At her direction, Jarrod kicked off his boots and peeled off his socks. Catie pushed his dress slacks down around his ankles and then whisked them aside when he stepped out of them.

Her fingers lightly skimmed over his cock as her teasing gaze met his. "Lie down on the bed." She ran her tongue over her lower lip. "Now, Sheriff."

His cock was at her mercy, and he wasn't about to argue. He eased onto the curtained four-poster bed and laid flat on his back, his hands behind his head, his cock practically standing straight up as he watched Catie remove her own clothing.

When she was naked, she scooped up the black scarf from the hardwood floor, where he'd dropped it earlier, then climbed onto the bed and straddled him, her pussy resting on his belly, his cock hitting her in the ass.

Jarrod eyed the scarf that she'd draped across his chest. "Planning to blindfold me?"

"Nah." She gave him a wicked smile. "I've got something a little different in mind. Now give me one of your arms."

He raised an eyebrow, but did as she asked. As she scooted off his chest, his mouth watered as he watched the jiggle of her small, perfect breasts, and her beautiful shaved mound. She pulled a silk cord from one bedpost by the headboard, releasing the curtain so that the bed was partially enclosed by frothy white material.

Obviously a woman who knew her knots, she quickly tied the end of the cord around his wrist, brushing his skin with the tassels. She then stretched his arm out and secured the opposite end of the rope to the bedpost.

"Uh, Catie?" He frowned, not sure if he should give her the opportunity to tie him up again. Well, the last time he'd been handcuffed. "What's going on in that pretty little head of yours?"

She'd already moved to the opposite bedpost and was repeating the same process with his other wrist. "Shush."

Jarrod lightly pulled against his bonds and found that she'd done a damn good job of it. He thought she was finished, but the next thing he knew, she was releasing the curtain at the footboard and securing the silk rope around his ankle, and then to the bedpost. She removed the last rope and then the curtains completely enclosed the bed, making it seem even more intimate.

He took deep breaths, watching her naked ass as she bent over. Her pussy gleamed with her juices and the urge to claim her was almost more than he could take.

When she finished tying him completely spread eagle, she knelt between his thighs and smiled. "I think I like having you at my mercy, Sheriff." She wrapped her fingers around his cock and rubbed her thumb over the top, wiping the drop of semen from the head, then licked his taste from her thumb. "Mmmmm. You taste like cream."

"I need to fuck you, Catie." His blood was a fire licking through his body.

"After I have my way with you." She reached for the black scarf still lying across his chest, and slid the silken material down his chest to his groin.

A groan rumbled from his chest as she slowly caressed his skin, and then wrapped the scarf around his raging cock. Her gaze was focused on his, studying him as he clenched his jaw while she rubbed the silk up and down his rod. "Do you like that?"

He could hardly think straight at that point, and talking wasn't real easy. "Honey. You keep that up and you're going to find out just how much."

Catie laughed, a husky sensual sound that caused the fire in his body to burn even hotter. She unwrapped the scarf from his cock, then moved up to straddle his hips again.

Good. She was about to put him out of his misery and fuck him. "Untie me," he demanded.

"Nope." With an ornery grin she moved her lips to his and kissed him. When he tried to deepen the kiss she pulled away. "I'm not finished with you yet."

Jarrod was real tempted to yank against those silken ropes, but he didn't want to ruin them. If Catie wasn't careful though, he'd say screw it and just owe Nicole a new set. He needed to get his hands on Catie. Needed to possess her in every way possible.

She pressed her lips to his ear and gently nipped his lobe before moving to his neck, licking and nipping him in light sensual bites. Her vanilla musk scent, and the smell of her juices intoxicated him, made him feel almost uncontrollable lust.

"I love your taste." She reached his chest and licked a path down the center. "I love your smile." Her pussy slid over his cock as she eased down his body, her mouth burning a trail as she went. "I love the way you look when I take your cock in my mouth and go down on you."

Her eyes met his as she grasped his erection in her palm. And then she slid her warm, wet mouth over his cock.

"Damn, Catie." Jarrod fought to hold back, his muscles straining against his bonds. "I can't hold off much longer."

The power she had over this man was heady and thrilling. Catie wanted Jarrod's cock in her pussy so bad she could almost scream, but she was enjoying this too much. Enjoying pleasuring him, making him as crazy for her as she was for him.

She slid his cock from her mouth and then nuzzled the soft hair around it. "I'll let you fuck me if you're real good, Sheriff."

"Untie me." His voice sounded strained, his jaw tight and his muscles bulging.

"When I'm good and ready." She cupped his balls in her hand and licked first one, and then the other.

"I'm about to ruin some nice ropes, honey." His body jerked as she licked his cock from base to head. "And I don't think Nicole would appreciate it."

"Wouldn't want to do that." She rubbed her breasts along his leg as she moved down and released one ankle. "And besides, I'm ready for you to fuck me."

"Hurry up, woman," Jarrod growled.

Catie smiled as she eased back up his body until she was straddling him, her pussy resting on his cock. She leaned forward, her nipples brushing his chest as she untied first one of his wrists and then the other.

The moment he was free, Jarrod flipped her on her back so fast that her head spun. "Damn what you do to me."

He lowered his head and captured her nipple in his mouth, licking and sucking it with such pressure that she thought the sensation was going to make her come. She buried her hands in his thick hair, pressing him closer as he moved his mouth to her other breast, nipping at it like something wild and untamed.

"Fuck me, Jarrod." She couldn't stand it anymore. She had to have his cock in her, filling her.

"After I taste you." He scooted down and pressed her thighs apart.

Catie arched her back, a cry tearing from her lips as he laved her pussy from top to bottom. She clenched her hands tighter in his hair, writhing beneath his mouth. Her whole body was burning for him and she felt like she might explode like a firecracker at any moment.

Jarrod rose up so that he was propped above her and positioned his erection at the entrance to her core. His mouth was wet with her juices, his eyes dark and sexy. "I love you Catie Savage," he said and then plunged his cock into her pussy.

She gasped at the intense sensation of him filling her. Knowing that he loved her as much as she loved him magnified the pleasure of their lovemaking.

Lovemaking. Not just fucking, it was making love.

His gaze remained focused on hers as he moved within her, his strokes slow and steady. For once she didn't need it hard and fast. She wanted it to last forever, to draw out this perfect moment.

Jarrod thrust firmly inside her, his balls slapping her ass. "Come with me, honey."

His words were like a visible stroke that shoved her over the edge just as his mouth claimed hers. He thrust his tongue in and out of her mouth as he fucked her, drawing out her climax.

A shudder tore through him as he came, his cock throbbing within her womb as he filled her with his semen. His body trembled against hers, and then he rolled to his side, keeping his cock snug inside her body, his mouth fastened to hers.

Tenderly her husband kissed her and then pulled back to look at her with love in those sexy green eyes. As she'd truly known all along they were meant for each other. That they would never make the same mistakes her parents had made.

Their love was forever.

"I love you, Jarrod Savage." She smiled and pressed her forehead to his. "And don't you ever forget that."

Epilogue

Jess Lawless nursed his beer as he studied the crowded recreation room of his cousin's bed-and-breakfast. Nicole had thrown one hell of a holiday party, and it looked like everyone in Bisbee had turned out for it.

With the practiced eye of a seasoned lawman, he studied the guests, automatically assessing and categorizing each individual as they danced or socialized. No doubt that couple making out in the corner would be trying to find someplace to fuck real soon. That or they'd be doing it right on the dance floor.

A brunette across the room had been making eyes at Jess for the last half hour, sticking her tits in his direction, her nipples hard and obvious through her thin dress. No doubt she'd be a willing roll in the hay.

Jess sighed and downed the last of his beer. He had no interest in women who were that obvious. A little chase was more interesting.

Hell, he didn't know what he really wanted anymore, just that he hadn't found it. Sure, he'd enjoyed the company of quite a few women, but he'd yet to come across one who could keep his attention for more than a night or two of good, hard sex. Not that it really mattered. Until he brought down this drug ring in Douglas, and captured that bastard Ryan Forrester, he was too busy for any kind of involvement.

He set his beer mug on a tray and glanced at the brunette again. Maybe a good fuck was what he needed before he headed back to the MacLeod Ranch and his undercover assignment.

Just as Jess got up from his stool and stood, Nicole walked down the stairs—but it was the woman beside Nicole who captured his attention. Nicole said something that caused the woman to laugh, and her lips curved into a radiant smile that met her beautiful green eyes.

Jess's sharpened senses took in every detail of the woman and came up with a puzzle. She appeared strong, sexy and confident, yet there was an air of innocence and vulnerability about her that made her something of a contradiction.

Intrigued, he watched her stroll into the room, her movements smooth and graceful. Her strawberry blonde hair was piled on top of her head in a sexy just-got-out-of-bed style, and her jade green eyes were big, giving her a wide-eyed look.

Yet the tiny red dress she wore was made for sin. It hugged her figure, showing her generous breasts, small waist and curvy hips. Definitely a dress designed to drive a man to his knees. And those high heels she was wearing—*damn*.

A vision came to him—having the woman beneath him, sliding between her thighs, filling her pussy with his cock while her desire-filled green eyes focused entirely on him.

Jess's groin tightened and he shifted his position.

Looked like this night might get real interesting.

"Too bad you're engaged," Nicole said as they walked down the stairs and into the rec room.

Tracilynn MacLeod laughed, while at the same time trying not to tumble down the staircase. She could just picture herself landing in a heap, this ridiculously tiny red dress up around her waist, exposing her thong underwear and garters.

"I'm not *exactly* engaged," Trace said, smiling at her friend as they reached the landing. "Harold just hinted, rather strongly, that he plans to ask me when he gets back to the states at Christmas."

Guiding Trace to the lavishly spread snack table, Nicole said, "Close enough."

Trace looked from the vat of red Christmas punch to the bottles of wine and decided on a white Zinfandel. At least that way if she spilled it on the carpet, it wouldn't stain like punch. She selected a wine glass and cocked an eyebrow at Nicole as she said, "I just told you that a man is going to ask me to marry him. Now why wouldn't you be happy for me?"

"My cousin." Nicole leaned close, and Trace caught her soft powdery scent. "The man is to die for, and if you were free, I know he'd rock your world."

Laughing, Trace rolled her eyes. "How do you know Harold doesn't rock my world?"

"Uh-huh." Nicole sniffed. "With a name like Harold, he no doubt wears a pocket-protector and horn-rimmed glasses."

Trace had just taken a sip of her wine and almost snorted it out her nose at the image of her boyfriend dressed like a stereotypical nerd. She could almost see it, which was the sad thing.

"Let me at least introduce you to Jess." Nicole put her hand on Trace's arm. "He's one gorgeous hunk of cowboy."

"Cowboy?" Trace shook her head. "I left that life four years ago. Even if I was free, and even if something ever came of it, I'm not about to settle down in the boonies. That was another life, another girl."

"Just—" Nicole started when the caterer rushed up and interrupted, saying Nicole was urgently needed upstairs in the kitchen.

"All right, all right." Nicole sighed and turned to Trace. "Will you be okay for a few minutes while I go handle this mini crisis?"

"Sure." Trace smiled and raised her wine glass. "I'll do my best to stay out of trouble."

When Nicole left, Trace lifted her glass to her lips and let her gaze drift over the people in the room. Music and laughter, sequins and glitter, Christmas lights and decorations.

Hair prickled at Trace's nape, as though she was being watched. Slowly she turned to see the most rugged, most handsome man she'd ever had the pleasure of viewing.

Standing directly behind her, inches away.

Instinctively she took a step back, but in a quick movement he caught her wrist, drawing her closer to him. Her flesh burned where he held her, and her mind went entirely blank.

The man's smile was so carnal that Trace's knees almost gave out. And those blue eyes—God, the way he was looking at her made her feel like he was making love to her right on the spot.

She tried to pull her wrist out of his grasp. "I—let go."

The man shook his head, the look in his eyes possessive and untamed. "No, sugar," he murmured, his sensual drawl flowing over her. "You're not going anywhere."

Enjoy this excerpt from
Forbidden
Seraphine Chronicles

Chapter One

Candlelight flickered across Liana's skin as the last of her clothing pooled at her feet. The scent of jensai blooms floated through the open window on an evening breeze, the balmy air easing over her body like a lover's caress.

Liana stood in the center of her bedchamber and closed her eyes, a vision of the dark stranger filling her senses. As she tilted her head back, her hair brushed her bare buttocks like a whisper of moonlight.

Like she imagined the man's touch would be upon her skin.

Even as she moved her hands to her naked breasts, she was aware of the nordai's passionate night calls outside her cottage. But the raven's cries faded as the stranger's image burned in Liana's thoughts.

Black eyes that had followed her as she had made her way through the tavern. Sensuality simmering beneath the surface of his stare. Ebony hair brushing his broad shoulders. A scruffy hint of a beard along his arrogant jaw. Muscles that flexed with every movement as he towered over her.

Visualizing the stranger's calloused hands upon her body, Liana caressed her taut nipples with her palms. She could almost smell the man's woodsy scent, a hint of which she had caught when she had brushed past him in the tavern. She had shivered from the slight contact, but kept her gaze averted, every nerve ending ablaze with wanting him.

How could she desire a man she had never seen before today?

How could she desire any man when it was *forbidden*?

A moan eased through Liana's lips as the vision of the stranger's touch grew stronger. She imagined his tanned fingers covering her pale breast, his calloused palm chaffing her sensitive nipples. She could feel the black hair on his powerful arms brushing her skin. Her body ached with desire, ached with need. A need she did not understand how to fill.

There was only one being with whom she was supposed to mate—but no. She would not allow that reality to spoil the erotic fantasy weaving through her mind.

She had never mated with a man, for it was forbidden. She had heard lusty tales told by her heart-sister Tierra and the tavern wenches, but Liana had never had such an intense desire to experience such a joining—

Until *him*.

Her belly quivered as she eased one hand down her flat stomach to the tangle of curls between her thighs. Where it was forbidden to touch herself. The place that now ached to be stroked, as though that might ease her wanting of the stranger.

Liana's tresses moved as an extension of her thoughts, sliding over her naked skin like she imagined the stranger might touch her body. His hands would be slow. Gentle. His mouth would feel hot on her lips, her breasts, her belly, leaving a trail of fire wherever he touched.

Burning.

Slipping her fingers between her folds, Liana gasped as she felt the dampness of her desire for the dark stranger. Her other hand continued to knead her nipples as she imagined the man fondling them. Her hair caressed her shoulders down to her hips, and the motion of her fingers grew stronger, more insistent, as she stroked her clit.

But instead of relieving her need for the man, the knot in her belly grew tighter and tighter yet.

She could almost feel the stranger's stubble, rough against her inner thighs. And his tongue—gods, his tongue—laving at her clit that was building with pressure. Building and building and—

A cry of surprise rose in Liana's throat and her eyes flew open as the most exquisite sensations rocked through her. Like a flock of startled blackbirds bursting from their roosts amongst the sacred vines. Like moonlight sparkling across the rainbow sands of Mairi.

Her fingers continued, drawing out the intense feelings until her body could take no more.

Liana dropped to her knees and braced her palms against the rush-covered floor, her hair swinging forward to cover her face. Her breasts swayed and her thighs trembled. Her breath came in short gasps as she struggled to overcome the dizziness that threatened to render her boneless.

When she had strength to move, Liana eased onto her haunches. A sound, ever so slight, pierced the haze still shrouding her confused mind. Through her curtain of hair, she glanced up to see an enormous ebony nordai perched on her windowsill, its black eyes focused intently on her—and a sheath was strapped to its powerful leg. The hilt of a dagger jutted out, a ruby glinting on its hilt like a drop of blood.

Ice chilled Liana's spine. *My gods — what have I done?*

* * * * *

Aric sucked in his breath as the Tanzinite maid collapsed to the floor with the strength of her orgasm. He had known he was breaching Liana's privacy when she had begun to shed her clothing—but he had been too enchanted to move.

And Lord Ir, when she had touched herself, he had nearly come undone. The flushed look of utter surprise and rapture on Liana's face when she had climaxed had been the most beautiful sight he had ever seen.

It had been all he could do to maintain his nordai form. Gods, how he had wanted to fly through her open window, resume his man's body and bury his cock inside her slit, claiming her virgin warmth and fucking her until she screamed her pleasure. How he wanted to be the cause of the ecstasy in those sea green eyes.

Forbidden.

She was of the Tanzinites, the cave-dwellers, and he of the Nordain, the Sky People. Never had the two races mated. Never would they.

Forbidden.

This was the woman who had been named to mate with the Sorcerer Zanden, a Nordain traitor. It was a joining Aric was sworn to prevent—by whatever means deemed necessary.

Forbidden.

The maid sat back upon her haunches, her breasts rising and falling with every breath, her flaxen hair shrouding her delicate features. She was a rare Tanzinite, born without wings, banished from the caves at birth and forced to live on Dair's surface amongst humans and fey folk.

Yet she was perfection. Candlelight danced across her silken skin, as beautiful as a Mairi pearl. Her nipples were the deep rose of the sacred vine's blossoms. The pale curls between her thighs like sea foam. And her hair, moonbeams spilling in shimmering waves past her hips.

His keen senses caught her scent as it rose up to him through the open window. Liana smelled of jensai blooms and moonlight. And of the passion between her thighs, a nectar of which he desired to drink his fill.

A lustful sound escaped Aric—and the maid's attention riveted on him. Even through her fine hair, he saw her sea green eyes widen with shock and fear. For a long moment their gazes remained locked, until Aric forced himself to move.

With a mighty flap of his wings, he took to the dark skies, trying to shove the erotic memories of the Tanzinite woman from his mind. He had a task to complete, and that did *not* include joining with the maid.

Though how in Lord Ir's name he would keep his hands off Liana, he did not know...

Enjoy this excerpt from
Wildcard
Wild

Chapter One

Tracilynn MacLeod peeked through the bedroom's filmy curtains and stared out into the drenched December evening. Goose bumps pebbled her skin, the colorful glow of Christmas decorations on each of the power poles somehow mesmerizing her. The sight brought back countless memories of her childhood, of celebrating the holidays in the desert. Some not-so-happy times, but she preferred to think about the ones that were joyous, or at least warm.

Below the B & B, the door of a classic old pickup truck swung open, and Trace watched as a man climbed out. In a fluid athletic motion he put on a dark cowboy hat and shut the door of the truck. With his long black duster swirling around his legs, he looked dark and dangerous, like an old west gunslinger who'd come to town to track down his prey.

The man tilted his head up, his face shadowed by the cowboy hat, and for a moment she could have sworn he was looking right at her. It was as though he could see through the curtain and straight through the tiny little dress her friend had talked her into wearing. Trace's heart pounded and her body had an instant reaction, her nipples hardening and her panties growing damp.

She swallowed hard, knowing she needed to back away from the window, to break the electric current that seemed to connect her to the mysterious cowboy, but she couldn't move.

"Trace, are you ready to come downstairs and join the party?" Nicole's voice sliced through that charged connection, snapping Trace's attention away from the man and to her friend.

"Just about." Trace cut her gaze to Nicole who was peeking through the bedroom door. "I need to fix my hair and that should do it."

"Here, let me help." Nicole bustled in, shutting the door behind her.

"Thanks." Trace moved away from the window and to the old-fashioned vanity mirror. She frowned at her reflection while she yanked down on the tiny skirt of the lipstick-red dress. "This is ridiculous," she muttered. The darn thing barely covered her ass, and her nipples poked against the silky material like mini torpedoes. And the neckline plunged halfway to her bellybutton, showing the full curve of her breasts from the inside for cripes sake. "I can't wear this to your Christmas party, Nic."

Trace turned from the mirror to glare at her best friend Nicole and pointed to the three-inch heeled sandals on her feet. "And where did you find these? If you had a better memory, you'd remember I'm a bit of a klutz."

"You're not a klutz. Well, maybe you used to be." Nicole's blue-green eyes glittered mischief. "And I'd say that dress was made for you. Those long legs, cute little butt…"

Trace snorted. "Stop looking at my butt."

"Can't help it." Nicole backed up, propped her hands on her full hips as she checked out Trace's figure. "I just can't get over how much you've changed in the last four years. No more glasses, and you're so…*tiny*. I didn't even recognize you when you first came to the door."

With a self-conscious smile, Trace studied her best friend since her first year at Cochise Community College, and on up through their fourth year at the University of Arizona. Before Trace had taken off for Europe, she and Nicole had been tighter than sisters...certainly closer than Trace had been to her real sister, Dee. Those last few years, anyway.

"It's all still a little weird to me." Trace raked her fingers through her hair as she spoke. "Having IntraLasik performed on my eyes was the best thing I've done for myself." She smiled. "Other than losing those ten dress sizes, that is."

Nicole cocked her head. "So how did you do it? The weight loss, I mean."

"Healthy eating." Trace shrugged. "I've also really gotten into kick-boxing, and all that exercise has made a world of difference for me."

"And what a difference." Nicole grinned. "Can't wait for our old classmates to get a load of you now. They'll flip."

"You'd think I'd be used to it." Trace smoothed her hands over the silky material of the dress and glanced down at her hips. "I've never had hip bones—well, not that I could ever see." She cut her eyes back to Nicole and pointed to her own shoulder. "And look at this. Shoulder bones!"

Nicole laughed and hugged Trace, her friendly embrace and soft baby powder scent bringing back memories of their college days. "I'm so proud of you, Trace." Nicole pulled away and smiled. "As far as I'm concerned, you've always been gorgeous. But now...*wow*. You're a knockout."

"Yeah, right." Trace turned back to the mirror and pushed her strawberry blonde hair on top of her head to see if it would look better up, and frowned at her reflection. The row of gold hoop earrings down her left ear glittered in the room's soft lighting. While she was in England, just to be different and a little quirky, she'd had five piercings done on her left ear, with only two on her left.

Trace sighed. "Dee's always been the beautiful one in the family."

A beauty that Trace had always envied as she was growing up. Dee had always been the prettiest, and certainly the thinnest. Dee had always won all the awards for barrel racing in every rodeo, and had even been a rodeo queen. And of course Dee had always made better grades.

Trace, well, she'd been the quiet one, all of her accomplishments hidden in the shadows. She'd been on the chunky side, with baby fat that turned into teenage fat and then adult fat—

A slap on Trace's ass jarred her from her thoughts. "Hey." She rubbed her stinging butt cheek with one hand and glared at Nicole over her shoulder. "You're not acquiring an ass fetish, are you?"

"No, dork." Shaking her head, Nicole scooped up a gold hairclip from the antique vanity table. "You've got to stop comparing yourself to your sister. Now sit." Nicole placed her hands on Trace's shoulders and firmly pushed her down onto the bench in front of the vanity mirror. "Look at all you've accomplished."

Trace shrugged. "No big deal."

Nicole narrowed her gaze at Trace's reflection. "Graduated with honors from U of A. Hired by Wildgames — only the best software company in the world. Never mind jetting all over Europe and shooting up the corporate ladder. Hell, you practically run Wildgames' Public Relations Department, and you've only been there four years." She gathered Trace's hair into the clip and didn't even stop for a breath. "And don't forget the best part. You're dating a company VP."

Trace knew better than to interrupt Nicole on a rant. The woman barreled along like a boulder rolling downhill when she had a point to make.

"And now you look incredible," Nicole finished as she fluffed the soft cloud of curls left out of the clip. "Like you walked out of *Cosmopolitan*."

Trace couldn't help but smile at her friend's enthusiastic support. "It's funny how confident and successful I've felt since I left home." Her smile faded a bit. "Until my airplane landed in Tucson. Now...I don't know. Time warp. I'm the old Trace instead of the new Trace."

"Close your eyes." Nicole held up the hairspray can.

Trace obeyed and held her breath as the spray hissed and a wet mist surrounded her. When she heard the can clunk on the dresser, she opened her eyes again and saw Nicole's reflection. She had her arms folded, her blue-green gaze focused on Trace in the mirror.

"You know what I see?" Nicole asked.

Trace gave her friend an impish grin as she waved away the lingering smell of melon-scented hairspray. "A redhead in a too-small red dress with no bra?"

"Turn." Nicole didn't even crack a smile as Trace slid around on the polished bench to face her friend.

"Now don't tell me." Trace scrunched her nose as though she was seriously considering Nicole's question. "A redhead with freckles?"

"I see the same Tracilynn MacLeod that I've known and loved." Nicole crouched so that she was eye level with Trace and rested her hands on the bench to either side of Trace's hips. "You've always been a butterfly, you just finally had a chance to come out of your cocoon."

Warmth rushed through Trace and she bit the inside of her lip before saying, "You're wonderful, you know that? You always know the right things to say."

Nicole adjusted the spaghetti strap of Trace's dress, a no-nonsense look on her pretty face. "Hush up and get that tiny ass downstairs. It's time to soar, Ms. Butterfly."

* * * * *

Jess hitched one hip against the bar while he nursed his beer and studied the crowded recreation room of his cousin's bed-and-breakfast. Nicole had thrown one hell of a holiday party, and it looked like everyone in Bisbee had turned out for it.

Nicole was a distant cousin on his mom's side of the family. He'd really just gotten acquainted with her since being on assignment for the DEA in this corner of Arizona. She knew he worked the area, and knew he was undercover, so she never asked questions about his work, which was just as well.

And if she'd get down here and join her own party, she might be able to point out a couple of the folks he'd heard would be here but didn't know by sight. Like that rich rancher's daughter, Kathy Newman, reportedly tight with Forrester at one time. Jess sighed and took another swig of beer. Damn. Guess he'd have to do a little of that mingling crap he hated.

With the practiced eye of a seasoned lawman, he studied the guests, automatically assessing and categorizing each individual as they danced or socialized. He'd bet his Stetson that couple making out in the corner would be trying to find someplace to fuck real soon. That or they'd be doing it right on the dance floor.

A good-looking gray-eyed brunette across the room had been making eyes at Jess, sticking her tits in his direction, her nipples hard and prominent through her thin black dress. No doubt she'd be a willing roll in the hay.

Jess sighed and tipped back his beer bottle for another swallow. He had no interest in women who were that obvious. A little chase was more interesting.

Hell, he didn't know what he really wanted anymore, just that he hadn't found it. Dee MacLeod had peaked his interest before Jake Reynolds had come back, but he'd never acted on it. Not to mention she'd originally been one of his chief suspects in the local trouble he'd been assigned to investigate.

And then there'd been Catie Wilds — a real spitfire — who would have sparked Jess's libido if she hadn't reminded him so much of his younger sister. He had to admit it was a surprise that anyone had been able to tame that wildcat, but Jarrod Savage had somehow managed to, and the more power to him. Hadn't left the sheriff as much time to pursue his former deputy, Ryan Forrester, but Jess supposed he was doing a fair job for a newly-married man.

Jess downed the last of his beer while he watched Jarrod Savage who was by the buffet table, talking to Ann O'Malley, a sexy cowgirl with brown hair and blue eyes, who owned a ranch just east of Bisbee. He could just imagine Catie kicking Jarrod's ass if she saw him talking to Ann, whether or not he was just being polite or investigating a lead.

The mellow malt flavor of the beer rolled down Jess's throat as he contemplated making a sexual conquest. It had been a little too long for his liking since he'd gotten laid. He'd enjoyed the company of quite a few women, but in the past few years he'd yet to come across one who could keep his attention for more than a night or two of good, hard sex.

Not that it really mattered. Until he brought down that drug ring infiltrating Douglas from Mexico, and until he got his hands around that turncoat bastard Forrester's worthless neck, he was too busy for any kind of involvement. Especially not the serious kind.

That whole cattle bullshit Forrester had arranged had just been a distraction, a sleight of hand, and a little more cash for the asshole. The real scheme involved smuggling drugs in from Mexico using illegal immigrants for mules. And that was where Rick McAllister of the Border Patrol had gotten involved in the investigation, and subsequently called on Jess.

Jess sure would like to know where that weasel Forrester was holed up. The men that Jarrod Savage, Jake Reynolds, and Jess had rounded up had been damn near worthless as far as information on the drug smuggling and Forrester's current hideout.

Gritting his teeth, Jess thumped his empty beer mug on a tray as he glanced at the brunette again. Maybe a good fuck was what he needed to get his head back in order before he headed back to the MacLeod Ranch and his undercover role as foreman. Hell, maybe that brunette would have some information he could fuck out of her.

Just as he pushed himself away from the bar, his cousin walked down the stairs—but it was the woman beside Nicole who captured his attention. Nicole said something that caused the woman to laugh, and her lips curved into a radiant smile that met her beautiful green eyes.

Eyes that seemed vaguely familiar to him. Yet he knew he'd never seen this woman before, and he never forgot a face. Ever.

Jess's sharpened senses took in every detail of the woman and came up with a puzzle. She appeared strong, sexy and confident, yet there was a contradicting air of vulnerability about her.

Intrigued, he watched her stroll into the room, her movements smooth and graceful. Her strawberry blonde hair was piled on top of her head in a sexy just-got-out-of-bed style, and her jade green eyes were big, giving her an innocent look.

Yet the tiny red dress she wore was made for sin. It hugged her figure, showing off her generous breasts, small waist and curvy hips. Definitely a dress designed to drive a man to his knees. And those high heels she was wearing—*damn*.

A vision came to him—having the woman beneath him, sliding between her thighs, filling her pussy with his cock while her desire-filled green eyes focused entirely on him.

Jess's groin tightened and he shifted his position.

Looked like this night might get real interesting.

"I'm going to have to hire a bodyguard just to beat the guys off of you," Nicole said as she and Trace headed down the stairs and into the enormous recreation room of the bed-and-breakfast. "You're a man magnet. I swear every male in this place is watching you." She pointed to the Doberman resting at the foot of the stairs. "Even Killer, my dog. Look at him staring at you — he's in love."

Trace laughed. "More than likely Killer just wants to sink his teeth into these stilts you call shoes," she said, while at the same time trying not to tumble down the staircase. She could just picture herself landing in a heap, this ridiculously tiny red dress up around her waist — now that would certainly get some attention.

Why had she let Nicole talk her into wearing this outfit, anyway? This was more Nicole's wild style than Trace's. The silver backless dress Nicole was wearing hugged her generous figure perfectly, outlining every beautiful curve. And the daring slit on one side went straight up to her hip bone. Nicole carried it off with elegance and style. Unlike Trace, Nicole never tripped or spilled anything.

Nicole greeted guests with a wave and a brilliant smile as they descended. "Too bad you're engaged," she said to Trace.

"I'm not *exactly* engaged." Trace gave a little shrug as they reached the landing. "Harold just hinted, rather strongly, that he plans to ask me when he comes to the States at Christmas."

Guiding Trace to the lavishly spread snack table, Nicole said, "Close enough. And it's a real shame."

Trace looked from the vat of red Christmas punch to the bottles of wine and decided on a white Zinfandel. At least that way if she spilled it on the carpet, it wouldn't stain. She selected a wineglass and cocked an eyebrow at Nicole as she said, "I just told you that a man is going to ask me to marry him. Now why wouldn't you be happy for me?"

"My cousin." Nicole leaned close, and Trace caught her powdery scent. "The man is to die for, and if you were free, I know he'd rock your world."

Laughing, Trace rolled her eyes. "How do you know Harold doesn't rock my world?"

"Uh-huh." Nicole sniffed. "With a name like Harold, he no doubt wears a pocket-protector and horn-rimmed glasses."

Trace had just taken a sip of her wine and just about snorted it out her nose at the image of her boyfriend dressed like a stereotypical nerd. Even though Harold was a devastatingly handsome man, with his reserved personality she could almost see him in that get-up. Her throat burned as she swallowed the wine and rolled her eyes at her friend.

"Let me at least introduce you to Jess." Nicole put her hand on Trace's arm. "He's one gorgeous hunk of cowboy."

"Cowboy?" Trace shook her head so hard it was a wonder her hair didn't tumble out of its clip. "I left that life four years ago. Even if I was free, and even if something ever came of it, I'm not about to settle down in the boonies. That was another life, another girl."

"Mmmm-hmmm." Nicole rolled her eyes. "You can take the cowgirl out of the country—"

"Trace, is that you?" a man's voice cut in, and Trace looked up to see Rick McAllister, one of the nicest as well as one of the most drop-dead gorgeous cowboys she'd ever known. At over six feet with that chestnut brown hair mussed all over his head, he looked like he'd just come in from a long trail ride. Sexy bastard.

"Rick!" Trace reached up and gave him a quick one-armed hug, being careful not to spill her wine. "Dang but it's good to see you."

"Well, hell. I hardly recognized you." He tweaked a tendril of Trace's hair and gave her his easy grin. "Probably wouldn't have if Nicole here hadn't told me you were coming. You're all grown up now."

Trace felt heat creep up her neck and she shook her head. "Thanks, big guy. You don't look so bad yourself." And he didn't. The tall, well-built man was a good eight years older than her, but she'd sure had a crush on him back when she was a teenager, until he'd gotten married. He'd always been more like a teasing older brother, and she'd come to appreciate him as a good friend. It had been a real shame when his wife was killed in that car accident, leaving him a widower and a single parent.

The faint ringing sound met her ears over the Christmas music. Rick gave Nicole and Trace a sheepish grin as he dug the phone out of his pocket and checked the caller ID. "Sorry, ladies. I'm on call and I've got to take this."

"No problem." Trace smiled and waved him off. "We'll do some more catching up later."

Rick nodded and put the phone to his ear as he headed up the stairs, probably to someplace where it was a little more quiet.

"You know that Rick's an intelligence agent with the Border Patrol, don't you?" Nicole's smile turned into a frown as she started to add, "He's here with—" she stopped as the caterer rushed up and interrupted, telling Nicole she was urgently needed upstairs in the kitchen.

"All right, all right." Nicole sighed and waved the caterer off. "Be right there." She turned to Trace. "Think you can fight off all the men while I go handle this mini crisis?"

"Sure." Trace laughed and raised her wine glass. "I'll do my best to stay out of trouble." Her gaze cut to Killer. "And I've got my buddy right here."

When Nicole left, Trace lifted the goblet to her lips and let her gaze drift over the party guests. It had been good to see Rick, as well as other old friends. Her thoughts turned to her first days back in the U.S., when she'd stayed a few days with another good friend, Lani Stanton. Two years ago, Lani had interviewed Trace about Wildgames, and they'd hit it right off. Lani was a journalist with a popular San Francisco magazine, but she was going through one hell of a messy divorce. Her ex-husband was a cheating bastard. Damn but Lani needed a good man.

Holiday music and laughter filled the room, and Trace smiled as she watched couples dancing to a country-western tune. The room glittered with all the women dressed in brilliant sequined dresses and from the hundreds of Christmas lights and decorations.

Scents of pine, cinnamon, and hot wine punch perfumed the air, along with the smell of burning mesquite wood in the fire blazing in the corner hearth. Sounds, sights, and smells of holidays that reminded Trace of growing up in Arizona, and made her feel like she was home.

Home...

No. Home was wherever Wildgames sent her. And home would be with Harold once he got around to asking her.

That was what she wanted, wasn't it? To marry Harold and continue rocketing to the top of the career ladder? They'd be good together, a match made in Wildgames Heaven.

Then why did the thought of living with Harold for the rest of her life make her feel trapped?

Jitters. Fear of commitment. That was it.

Hair prickled at Trace's nape, as though she was being watched, and a slight shiver skittered down her spine. Slowly she pivoted and came to an abrupt stop. She caught her breath at the sight of the most rugged, most handsome cowboy she'd ever had the pleasure of viewing.

He'd been standing directly behind her, inches away.

Instinctively she took a step back, but in a quick movement he caught her wrist, drawing her closer to him. Her flesh burned where he held her, and her mind went entirely blank.

The man's smile was so carnal that Trace's knees almost gave out. And those blue eyes—God, the way he was looking at her made her feel like he was making love to her right on the spot.

She clutched her wine glass between them as she tried to pull her wrist out of his iron grasp. "I—let go."

The man shook his head, the look in his eyes possessive and untamed. "No, sugar," he murmured, his sensual Texan drawl flowing over her. "You're not going anywhere."

About the author:

Cheyenne McCray is a thirty-something wild thing at heart, with a passion for sensual romance and a happily-ever-after...but always with a twist. A University of Arizona alumnus, Chey has been writing ever since she can remember, back to her kindergarten days when she penned her first poem. She always knew that one day she would write novels, and with her love of fantasy and romance, combined with her passionate nature, erotic romance is a perfect genre for her. Cheyenne's books have won numerous awards, including "Best Erotic Novel of the Year," by the Romantic Times BOOKclub, The Road to Romance's "Reviewer's Choice Award," Romance Reviews Today's "Perfect 10 Award," and the CAPA for "Best New Author."

In addition to her adult work, Chey is also published in young adult literary fiction under another name. Chey enjoys spending time with her husband and three sons, traveling, working out at the health club, playing racquetball, and of course writing, writing, writing.

Cheyenne welcomes mail from readers. You can write to her c/o Ellora's Cave Publishing at 1337 Commerce Drive, Suite 13, Stow OH 44224.

Why an electronic book?

We live in the Information Age—an exciting time in the history of human civilization in which technology rules supreme and continues to progress in leaps and bounds every minute of every hour of every day. For a multitude of reasons, more and more avid literary fans are opting to purchase e-books instead of paperbacks. The question to those not yet initiated to the world of electronic reading is simply: *why?*

1. *Price.* An electronic title at Ellora's Cave Publishing runs anywhere from 40-75% less than the cover price of the <u>exact same title</u> in paperback format. Why? Cold mathematics. It is less expensive to publish an e-book than it is to publish a paperback, so the savings are passed along to the consumer.

2. *Space.* Running out of room to house your paperback books? That is one worry you will never have with electronic novels. For a low one-time cost, you can purchase a handheld computer designed specifically for e-reading purposes. Many e-readers are larger than the average handheld, giving you plenty of screen room. Better yet, hundreds of titles can be stored within your new library—a single microchip. (Please note that Ellora's Cave does not endorse any specific brands. You can check our website at www.ellorascave.com for customer

recommendations we make available to new consumers.)

3. *Mobility*. Because your new library now consists of only a microchip, your entire cache of books can be taken with you wherever you go.

4. *Personal preferences are accounted for*. Are the words you are currently reading too small? Too large? Too…**ANNOYING**? Paperback books cannot be modified according to personal preferences, but e-books can.

5. *Innovation*. The way you read a book is not the only advancement the Information Age has gifted the literary community with. There is also the factor of what you can read. Ellora's Cave Publishing will be introducing a new line of interactive titles that are available in e-book format only.

6. *Instant gratification.* Is it the middle of the night and all the bookstores are closed? Are you tired of waiting days—sometimes weeks—for online and offline bookstores to ship the novels you bought? Ellora's Cave Publishing sells instantaneous downloads 24 hours a day, 7 days a week, 365 days a year. Our e-book delivery system is 100% automated, meaning your order is filled as soon as you pay for it.

Those are a few of the top reasons why electronic novels are displacing paperbacks for many an avid reader. As always, Ellora's Cave Publishing welcomes your questions and comments. We invite you to email us at service@ellorascave.com or write to us directly at: 1337 Commerce Drive, Suite 13, Stow OH 44224.

Discover for yourself why readers can't get enough of the multiple award-winning publisher Ellora's Cave. Whether you prefer e-books or paperbacks, be sure to visit EC on the web at www.ellorascave.com for an erotic reading experience that will leave you breathless.

WWW.ELLORASCAVE.COM

Printed in the United States
93686LV00001B/268-303/A